IT'S THE FIRST DAY OF SCHOOL... FOREVER!

IT'S THE FIRST DAY OF SCHOOL... FOREVER!

R.L. STINE

SQUARE FISH
FEIWEL AND FRIENDS
NEW YORK

FOR JEAN,

WHO ALWAYS HAS THE SCARIEST IDEAS

SQUARE
FISH

An Imprint of Macmillan

 Printed in the United States of America by
R. R. Donnelley & Sons Company, Harrisonburg, Virginia. For information,
address Square Fish, 175 Fifth Avenue, New York, NY 10010.

Library of Congress Cataloging-in-Publication Data

Stine, R. L.
It's the first day of school— forever! / R. L. Stine.
p. cm.
Summary: Everything goes wrong for eleven-year-old Artie on his first day
at Ardmore Middle School, from the moment his alarm goes off until the
next morning, when everything is repeated exactly the same way.
ISBN: 978-1-250-00476-5
[1. First day of school—Fiction. 2. Schools—Fiction.
3. Monsters—Fiction. 4. Horror stories.] I. Title.
II. Title: It is the first day of school—forever!
PZ7.S86037Its 2011
[Fic]—dc22
2010050896

Originally published in the United States by Feiwel and Friends
First Square Fish Edition: May 2012
Square Fish logo designed by Filomena Tuosto
Book designed by Elizabeth Tardiff
mackids.com

4 6 8 10 9 7 5 3

AR: 3.2 / LEXILE: 400L

DAY ONE

1

My name is Artie Howard, and here goes. Here is the worst day of my life.

What could be worse than today?

Well, imagine that you have a dentist appointment. The dentist has to drill a big hole in your tooth. And he keeps drilling and drilling and drilling. For hours.

Imagine what that feels like. The dentist never takes a break. He just keeps grinding and drilling, grinding and drilling, deeper and deeper, until he drills right into your brain.

Are you feeling it? Are you imagining that?

Well . . . my day was worse than that. Much worse.

Forget about the dentist. That's small-time trouble. Don't even think about the dentist. I've got a much more painful story to tell.

The morning started with a *lot* of pain. The alarm went off, and I fell out of bed.

My head hit the wood floor and bounced once or twice. I actually saw stars, just like in the cartoons.

I'd been sound asleep. But I was wide awake now, trying to blink away the pain that throbbed through my head. And trying to make the room stop spinning.

Before I could pull myself up, Mom walked into my room.

"Artie, what are you doing down on the floor?"

"Just my morning exercises," I said.

Okay, okay. I'm a bit of a wise guy. A good sense of humor never hurt anyone, right?

Dad says I have a "smart mouth." He doesn't mean it to be nice. But I'd rather have a smart mouth than a *dumb* mouth—wouldn't you?

"You don't have time for exercises," Mom said. "It's the first day of school, remember?"

I groaned. "I think you reminded me of that a few hundred times."

Mom helped pull me to my feet. She squinted at me. "How did you get that bump on your head?"

"Just lucky," I said. I rubbed it. It hurt. So I stopped rubbing it.

Mom started picking up the clothes I'd tossed on

the floor the night before. She can be very helpful that way.

She smiled at me. "I hope you like your new school."

Mom has a great smile. Actually, she may be the best-looking mom ever. She has white-blonde hair and bright blue eyes and dimples in her cheeks when she smiles.

She says she was a fashion model after college. But she likes to eat, so she had to give it up.

My whole family likes to eat. A lot. Which may explain why all four of us are *not* tiny people.

You might say we're kind of chubby. But that would be rude.

I blinked a few more times. I was still a little dizzy from hitting my head on the floor.

"My new school?" I said. "Aardvark Middle School?"

"It's not Aardvark. It's Ardmore," Mom said. "Why do you keep calling it that?"

"Because it's funny?" I said.

"Funny won't get you a loaf of bread," Mom said. It's one of her expressions. Don't ask me what it means.

I just know Mom doesn't like funny. She and Dad are both pretty serious. They're both economics professors at the community college. That's kind of serious.

She left carrying an armload of dirty clothes.

"Don't forget you have a dentist appointment after school," she called from the hallway.

"I already forgot!" I shouted back.

She thinks eleven-year-olds don't have a memory. That *has* to be why she reminds me of everything a dozen times.

"Bring your cell phone," Mom said. "Take the bus to the dentist and call me when you get there."

"Aye, aye," I said.

Okay. Time to get dressed. What should I wear to impress my new friends at Aardvark?

I'm not going to pretend that I haven't been thinking about it nonstop.

In fact, two night ago, I pulled out all my T-shirts and spread them across my bed. Which one should I wear? Which one?

I decided the shirt had to be black. Black is the only cool color. My eyes wandered over the black T-shirts, reading the words on the fronts:

THANKS FOR SHARING

LOL

I ROCK

YOUR FAVORITE BAND SUCKS

STAND BACK. WIDE LOAD

Definitely *not* the last one. Who *gave* me that shirt?

I settled on a black shirt with red letters that

simply said: T-SHIRT. It wasn't that funny. But at least it wasn't embarrassing.

I pulled the T-shirt down over my raggediest stonewashed faded straight-legged jeans with rips in both knees. Then I fought down my insanely curly springy black hair.

Every time I brush it down, it pops right back up. Like *boinnnng*. I battle my hair every morning, and I always lose.

Oh, well. Ready to rock and roll.

I picked up my phone and glanced at the screen. No text messages or missed calls. Could that be because I don't know anybody here?

The little battery in the corner of the screen was blinking. I'd forgotten to power up the thing.

Oh, well. Plenty of time while I was having breakfast.

I found the charger. Stuck it into the phone. Then I jammed the plug into the outlet near my floor. And . . .

Zzzzzzzzzzaaaaaaap.

2

Guess who got the blast of roaring electricity jolting through his body?

Did you guess Artie Howard?

I did a crazy dance around my room. My sneakers drummed the floor like a tap dancer in fast-forward. I couldn't control my arms or legs.

When the pain finally stopped, it left me with a loud buzz in my ears. And was I dizzy? In a word, *uh-huh*.

I had to brush down my hair again. It was standing straight up on end.

Then I stumbled down the stairs to the kitchen for breakfast.

I saw a dirty plate at Dad's place, so I knew he had already left for work. Mom was at the coffeemaker near the sink. Wowser was under the table, hoping for some food to drop on the floor.

We call Wowser our Everything Dog. He's mostly yellow Lab and shepherd with Everything Else thrown in. One day, an entire lamb chop fell off the table right in front of Wowser. He's been waiting under the table ever since.

My little brother Eddy sat at the table, a tall stack of toaster waffles in front of him.

I say that Eddy is my little brother, but he isn't exactly little. Everything about him is round, mainly his face and his body. He has springy black hair just like me and Dad. But he has Mom's round blue eyes, which give him a real baby face.

Don't be fooled. Eddy is not a sweet little baby. He's okay, but you don't really want to get too close to him. For one thing, he bites.

Yes, he's five. But he still likes to bite.

Mom thinks it's cute. But I'm really afraid he's going to give me *rabies*.

You also want to watch out for Eddy because he's a total klutz. He swings his round body and waves and gestures with his hands when he talks.

He's always bumping into things and knocking everything over and spilling anything within ten feet of him. For a lumpy little guy, he has amazing reach!

It's like he has rubber arms! He can reach all the way across the table and grab food off my plate.

Anyway, I sat down across from him at the kitchen table. He swung his hand and spilled his orange-juice glass. The juice trickled onto my side of the table and started to drip over the side.

"Hey—" I jumped to my feet. *No way* I wanted orange-juice stains on my worst pair of jeans. It had taken a long time to make my worst pair of jeans perfect, and I didn't want them messed up.

Eddy laughed. Actually, he giggled. Like a mad scientist in the cartoons.

Mom came running over with a dish towel to mop up the juice. "Eddy, don't laugh. It isn't funny," she said.

That made him giggle some more.

"You spill more juice than you drink," Mom said.

"Maybe I don't like juice," he said in his whiny little baby voice. He has a smart mouth, too.

When the table was dry, I sat back down. "Eddy, you know you weren't born," I said. "You were picked out of somebody's nose."

"Artie, don't be gross," Mom said.

"Just telling the truth," I said.

"Is that how babies are born?" Eddy said. He was just being stupid.

The toaster at the end of the table popped. *Boinnnnng*. The waffles shot up into the air. I swiped them and dropped them onto my plate.

I reached for the syrup bottle. Eddy reached for it, too. "More syrup," he said.

He squeezed the bottle. Thick brown syrup made a *thwuppp* sound as it sprayed from the plastic bottle—shot across the table—and splashed into my hair.

At first, I didn't believe it. But then I felt the sticky goo sliding down the side of my head.

"Mom!" I screamed. I reached my hand up and brushed it along my hair. Now my hand was sticky and wet.

Eddy giggled. "Oops," he said. He never says he is sorry about anything. All he ever says is "Oops."

The whole left side of my hair was glued together. "Mom—look what he did!" I cried.

"I see," Mom said. "That's a sticky mess." She frowned at Eddy. "Why did you do that to your brother?"

"Oops." Eddy said it again.

Mom thinks he's so adorable. He always gets away by saying *Oops*.

I jumped to my feet. "I . . . I have to go wash the syrup out of my hair," I said.

Mom glanced at the brass clock shaped like a frying pan above the sink. "No time," she said. "You don't want to be late for your first day in a new school."

"I don't want to be a glue-haired geek my first day in a new school!" I cried.

"It's on your shirt, too," Eddy said, pointing.

Yes. Nice one, Eddy. Gooey syrup down one sleeve.

"I'm sorry," Mom said. "Go take a towel and try to rub it out as best you can."

Before I could move, Wowser jumped up, plopped his big paws on my shoulders—and began to lick the syrup off my shirt sleeve.

"Let go! Let go of me, Wowser!" The dog's tongue was as big as my hand.

RRRRRIPPPPP.

His nails shredded the sleeve of my T-shirt. I finally pushed him away and started to my room. "Breakfast went well," I told myself. "Good start to the day."

I ran upstairs. I pulled off the T-SHIRT T-shirt. I put on my black T-shirt with the yellow-chalk outline of a body. It looks just like the crime-scene drawings on TV.

Maybe it was a little *bold* for the first day of school. But what choice did I have? I couldn't wear a T-shirt with LOL on the front. Everyone would laugh at me.

In the bathroom, I tried to brush the syrup from my hair. But the hairbrush stuck to my head.

Think fast, Artie. I had to do something. I grabbed a blue-and-red Cubs cap from my closet and pulled it down over my hair.

That looked a lot better. My first day in a new school. Of course, I wanted to make a good impression. All I cared about was looking cool.

"Hurry, Artie," Mom shouted from downstairs. "You're going to be late."

"Coming," I shouted back. I checked myself out in the mirror one more time. Then I started down the stairs.

Mom was waiting at the bottom of the stairs. "Oh. By the way," she said. "You have to walk Eddy to his kindergarten."

"Yaaaaay," Eddy cheered and stomped as hard as he could on my foot.

Pain shot up my leg. I slung my backpack over my shoulder and limped out of the house, dragging my aching foot.

"And hold Eddy's hand when crossing the street," Mom called.

Oh, yeah. I was *definitely* going to look cool.

3

It had rained hard the night before. The sky was still gray with streaks of morning yellow breaking through. The street and sidewalk were filled with big puddles of rainwater.

Eddy insisted on jumping into all of them.

"Stop it! You're splashing me!" I shouted.

That made him giggle. He leaped into a wide puddle with both feet. His sneakers were soaked, but he didn't seem to care. He only cared about making big splashes.

"Ba-boom! Ba-boom! Ba-boom!" he cried out with each splash.

I tried to stay as far away from him as I could.

I saw several other kids walking to school. I didn't want them to know that this jumping chimpanzee was part of my family.

But I had to hold his hand when we crossed streets. If I didn't, he'd tell Mom.

Eddy got such a thrill from snitching on me.

His school was only three blocks from our house. But with him dancing and jumping and splashing, it seemed like three *miles*.

"Ba-boom! Ba-boom! Ba-boom!"

"Stop splashing. Can't you *walk*?" I demanded.

"No," he replied. "I can only jump." He leaped into a muddy puddle and sent water flying around him.

Aardvark Middle School was two more blocks down the street. Could I drop Eddy off at the door and make it to my new school safely?

No.

We stepped up to the corner across from his school. It was a long, one-story brick building with a grassy playground at the side. On a tall pole near the entrance, an American flag flapped against the gray sky.

A big black-and-yellow sign near the front walk read: CYRUS ELEMENTARY, HOME OF THE FIGHTING BUMBLEBEES.

Eddy grabbed my T-shirt sleeve. "What does that sign say?" he asked.

"It says *Big Baby School*," I told him. "That's the name of your school. Big Baby School."

"It does not!" he cried.

I was about to reply when the truck came roaring by.

It was one of those long silver-tank trucks with the word GASOLINE on the side. It thundered past us. Its engine roared like a wild animal.

The big tires shot through a wide puddle—sending a huge tidal wave of water over the sidewalk.

I felt a splash of cold on the front of my jeans.

With a gasp, I glanced down.

The front of my jeans was soaked through.

My mouth dropped open. It happened so quickly. I just stared at the big, dark stain on the front of my jeans.

Then I heard Eddy start to laugh like a maniac.

"It looks like you *peed*!" he cried.

4

I took Eddy into his school and dropped him off in his classroom. His teacher had bright red hair and a lot of freckles.

She said, "Hi and welcome" to my brother. But she was staring at the front of my jeans the whole time.

At least, I thought she was.

I tried to tug the bottom of my T-shirt down over the wet stain. But the T-shirt was too short.

Why were my jeans taking so long to dry?

I tried to walk slowly to my school to give them time to dry. But I didn't want to be late. Other kids were hurrying past me. I could swear each one stopped to stare at the wet spot on my jeans.

But maybe it was my imagination.

Ardmore Middle School looks more old-fashioned

than my brother's Big Baby School. His school looks like a long ranch house. My school looked like a school you see in old movies on TV.

It was a tall, gray stone building with lots of windows up the front of its four floors. Ivy creeps down from the roof and dangles over nearly half the front wall.

I saw a teachers' parking lot filled with cars. Behind it—a small football stadium with bleacher seats on both sides. Some kids were tossing a baseball back and forth on the sidewalk at the bottom of the front steps.

I glanced down at my jeans. Still wet.

With a sigh, I started to climb the stone steps that led to the white double doors at the entrance. I was halfway up when I recognized the man in the brown suit at the top.

He was Mr. Jenks, the principal. I'd met him when Mom and Dad brought me to see my new school for the first time. He was shaking hands and greeting every student.

Mr. Jenks was a smiley kind of guy. He had a round, bald head and tiny blue eyes, and he always seemed to have a smile on his face. Like it was painted or glued on or something.

His eyes, nose, and mouth were jammed in the

middle of his face. When I first saw him, I thought of Mr. Potato Head.

But he seemed like a nice guy. And his smile was a kind smile.

He stared right at you with those little blue eyes, like he was really interested in what you were saying. And he had a soft voice—very calm.

I only met him that one day last summer. But he seemed much nicer than my old principal, who liked to act tough and give orders.

"Artie, hello," he said. He reached out and shook my hand. I smelled peppermint on his breath. "Welcome to Ardmore."

Was he staring at the wet stain on my jeans?

Two girls passed by. They both looked at my jeans. I know they did.

Mr. Jenks adjusted the collar of the yellow turtleneck he wore under the brown suit jacket. "First, you need to find whose class you are in," he said. "The class lists are posted on the wall across from my office."

"Thank you," I said. I started to step past him, but he stopped me.

"Artie, I'm sorry. We don't wear baseball caps in this school. Could you take yours off?"

"Uh . . . sure," I said.

I grabbed the bill of the cap and started to tug. I was surprised when the cap didn't slide off easily. It was stuck.

Then I remembered why I was wearing the cap. Syrup hair!

I had no choice. I gave the cap a hard tug—and let out a sharp cry. A massive chunk of my hair came off with the cap.

That syrup was worse than glue. Now I had a big bald spot on the side of my head.

I tried to straighten what was left of my hair. But it was matted in sticky, stiff clumps.

Well, okay. I was not exactly going to be the coolest looking dude in the sixth grade today.

"Look out!" someone shouted from the bottom of the stairs. A baseball bounced off the wall near my head.

I turned to see a blond-haired kid in a pale blue sweatshirt. "Sorry," he said. He picked up the baseball and tossed it to his friend across the grass.

Mr. Jenks was saying hello to twin girls, who were both laughing hard about something he'd said. Covering the side of my hair with one hand, I stepped into the school.

I was nearly through the front door when I heard a commotion behind me.

Kids shouted.

A dog barked.

"Huh?" I spun around—and instantly recognized the big dog racing up the stairs.

"Wowser?"

Oh, no. He followed me to school.

"Wowser—down!" I shouted.

But the dog never listens to me.

I watched helplessly as the giant monster dog—*my* giant monster dog—stretched onto his hind legs. Leaped onto Mr. Jenks. Licked the principal's face. Pawed his shoulders, leaving big mud stains all over.

Then I heard a loud *rrrripppp* as Wowser tore the jacket pocket right off the principal's brown suit.

Mr. Jenks' face turned bright red. "Artie," he said softly. "Is this your dog?"

5

Mr. Jenks stood there red-faced. His jacket had black paw prints across the front. He held the ripped pocket limply in one hand.

Wowser wagged his furry yellow tail furiously. I think he had a big grin on his face. It's hard to tell with dogs.

But he seemed very pleased with himself.

"I—I guess he followed me," I stammered.

Mr. Jenks was very kind about the whole thing. In fact, the smile quickly returned to his face.

"He must have smelled my dog," he said. He stuffed the ripped pocket into his pants pocket.

Was I totally embarrassed by the whole thing?

Does Wowser have fleas? Yes. I wanted to sink into a deep rain puddle and never come up for air.

I grabbed the big dog by his leather collar. "I'll take him home," I told the principal.

"That's okay," Jenks said. "You don't want to be late for class on the first day."

He leaned down and petted Wowser under the chin. Then he took hold of the dog's collar.

"Is your mom or dad home?" he asked.

"Mom," I said.

"Well, I'll call her and ask her to pick up the dog," Jenks said.

Wowser licked the principal's hand. He left a big gob of saliva on Jenks' wrist. "Go find your class, Artie. I'll take care of your dog."

I didn't wait for him to change his mind. I hurried into the front hall.

The school was ten times bigger than my old school. The hall seemed to stretch for miles, with gray lockers down both sides. It was so long, I couldn't see the end. Like it went to another *state* or something!

A tall glass trophy case was filled from top to bottom with silver sports awards. A sign inside the case read, GO, OTTERS!

A red-and-white banner stretched across the hall. It had glittery musical notes all over it and read, ARDMORE ROCKS YOUR WORLD.

Kids jammed the front hall. They stared at the long sheets of computer printouts taped to the yellow-tile wall. Kids pushed and elbowed their way to the front to read what class they were in.

I shifted the backpack on my shoulders and moved into the crowd. My hair itched. I scratched it without thinking and got my fingers all sticky.

I glanced down the long front hall. Door after door of classrooms and other rooms.

Where were they numbered? Were different grades on different floors? How would I ever find the gym or the lunchroom—or the boys' room?

These are the questions you have when you start a new school. I think it was even tougher for me because I didn't know a single kid in the school.

I didn't realize I was about to meet someone—about to make my first *enemy*.

6

"Yo, Brick! Brick!"

A tall, skinny boy with spiky blond hair yelled in my ear. I stepped away. He pushed past me toward a big guy in a red-and-white football jersey. The jersey had the number "1" on the back and front.

"Yo, Brick! Did you get McVie?" the skinny boy yelled.

The kid named Brick swung around. He *looked* like a brick: big and solid and kind of square-shaped, with a football player's thick neck and shoulders.

He had wavy brown hair and big brown eyes. A nice smile.

"Hey, Brick," another kid shouted. "I'm in your class. We both got Freeley."

Brick touched knuckles with the kid. Other kids

reached their fists out. It looked like everyone wanted to touch knuckles with Brick.

He was a real good-looking dude. And he seemed to be very popular.

I couldn't read the class lists. I tried to push my way closer.

Brick turned and started to walk away with the kid with spiky hair. I tripped over someone's foot—stumbled—and landed hard on Brick's foot.

"Hey—" He let out a startled cry. Then he groaned. "Oww."

He raised his brown eyes to me. That nice smile of his disappeared. "Dude, you're even heavier than you look," he said. He took a few limping steps.

"S-sorry," I stammered.

The spiky-haired kid stared at the front of my jeans. "Do you have to use the bathroom or something?"

I heard some kids laugh. I could feel my face growing hot.

I'm an easy blusher. Everyone in my family is an easy blusher. It's so totally embarrassing. But what can you do about it?

Brick and the other kid headed down the hall.

"You'd better go apologize to Brick," a voice beside me said.

I turned to see a girl in a bright yellow top and a short brown skirt.

She had straight black hair down to her shoulders and huge gray-green eyes.

She was totally *hot.* I mean, she looked like she could be a model or on TV or something.

"Excuse me?" I said.

"You'd better tell Brick you're sorry," she said. "He rules this school."

"He does?"

My brain was spinning. I couldn't think of how to say words. I'd never stood so close to a girl this totally awesome.

"Well, you know. He's an all-state middle school quarterback," the girl said. "And he's totally a good guy. And he's a brain. Everyone likes him."

I tried to talk, but I made a clucking sound. Like a chicken.

"What's your name?" I managed to choke out.

She tossed back her shiny black hair with a shake of her head. "Shelly."

I blinked. "You mean, like short for *Sheldon*?"

"No. Michelle," she said. She squinted at me. Like she was thinking, *What planet do you come from?*

I started to ask her what class she was in. But I didn't have a chance. Because I heard kids shout—and that baseball came flying through the front door.

I caught it in both hands.

I didn't mean to catch it. I didn't even think about it. I'm not a good catch. I'm terrible at sports.

Well . . . I'm a pretty good volleyball player. Because you don't have to run around a lot.

Anyway, I caught the ball. A few kids cheered. That made me feel good.

But this wasn't my day to feel good.

I heard a shout. "Throw it here!" It was the spiky-haired kid down the hall with Brick.

He raised his hands. "Yo, dude—throw it here!" he shouted.

I pulled back my arm and heaved the ball.

I knew right away that my aim wasn't good. I felt the ball slip as I threw it.

I could see it. I could see what was going to happen. And as I watched helplessly, I felt a heavy knot of dread in the pit of my stomach.

The ball sailed down the hall. It made a very loud *thwoccck* as it hit Brick in the back of the head.

"Oohhhhh." A weird moan escaped his throat.

His arms shot straight up. He did a weird tap dance. Then his knees folded. And he sank to the floor, unconscious.

7

Kids screamed. Everyone stampeded down the hall toward him.

I froze. My breath caught in my throat.

This isn't happening. This isn't happening.

I let out a long sigh of relief when Brick finally sat up. He rubbed the back of his head. He gazed around, blinking.

"Who threw that ball?" he demanded.

The spiky-haired kid pointed at me.

I hadn't moved from the spot where I'd thrown the ball. Everyone stared.

Tense. Tense moment.

I felt cold sweat on the back of my neck.

Brick rubbed his head some more. He squinted at me. "Dude—was that a fastball or a curve?"

Squeals of laughter echoed off the tile walls. Two

guys helped Brick to his feet. He shook his head hard and took a few steps. He seemed okay.

"S-sorry," I said. "It slipped."

But no one was paying attention to me anymore. They were all gathered around Brick. Joking and laughing and happy that he was okay.

I took a deep breath and let it out slowly. I knew I wasn't the most popular kid in school at that moment.

But it could have been worse—right?

I found my name on the class lists. I had Ms. McVie in Room 307.

Okay. Step One accomplished. Now for Step Two: *Find* Room 307.

This sounds easy but it wasn't. The halls seemed to stretch on forever in this school. And the room numbers were etched on tiny brass signs in the middle of the doors. Impossible to read unless you stuck your nose right up to them.

Also, the numbers were all crazy. Room 107 was followed by 134.

It was getting late. The halls were nearly empty. Voices rang out from all the classrooms.

I passed a big auditorium. Then another long hall of classrooms. Finally, I found the stairs. My shoes rang out as I trotted to the second floor. Only a few other stragglers still in the hall.

You would think that the 300 numbers would be on the third floor. But you would be wrong.

Room 301 was right next to Room 201. And the next room didn't even have a number on the door.

The sign on the next door said "412." I looked through the window—and gasped. There wasn't a room behind the door. Just blue sky.

If you opened the door and took a step, you'd fall straight down to the ground.

What kind of school was this? Shouldn't there be a warning sign?

I spun away and walked past a few doors. Did I go the wrong way? Did I pass my room somehow? Was I on the right floor for Room 307?

I had this tight choking feeling in my throat. I felt a little sick to my stomach.

I hated being the new kid. Everyone else probably found their rooms with their eyes closed.

I stared down the long hall. Empty. No one to help me.

I turned the corner. Room 306 was the first door. "Yesss!" I started to feel a little better.

The bell rang as I stepped into the next classroom. The room was filled with laughing, talking kids. They looked my age, sixth graders.

One kid, a pudgy, round-faced dude in a long

orange T-shirt with two grinning M&M'S on the front stood on a window ledge and did a crazy dance. Kids clapped and cheered him on.

Yep. Sixth graders.

I glanced around, searching for Ms. McVie. No sign of her. I guessed the kid wouldn't be doing his dance if the teacher was in the room.

My eyes scanned the desks. They were all taken. Oh, wait. I spotted one empty desk near the back of the room.

I pulled off my backpack and dropped into the seat behind the desk.

On the window ledge, the M&M'S kid finished his dance. He took a deep bow, then jumped down.

I reached into my backpack and started to pull out a writing pad.

Something in the pack was all sticky. I pulled my hand out. Two fingers stuck together.

Did Eddy spill syrup into my backpack, too?

I didn't have time to investigate. A dark shadow fell over me.

I sat up—and stared at Brick. Actually, I was staring at the big number "1" on his jersey.

He stood over me, breathing hard. He wasn't smiling.

"Are you *following* me?" he demanded.

"Uh . . . no," I said.

"Then why are you in my seat?" he said. "Get up, dude. This is my desk."

He put a hand on my shoulder. Was he going to *pull* me up from the desk?

That's when the teacher walked in.

8

The teacher was an older woman with very short gray hair, pale gray eyes, and pale cheeks. She wore a gray cardigan sweater over loose-fitting gray slacks.

She was so short and gray, she *had* to be part mouse!

Brick still had his hand on my shoulder. I stood up and dragged my backpack away so he could sit down. He deliberately bumped me as he dropped into the seat.

"Ms. McVie, there aren't enough seats," I said.

"I'm not Ms. McVie," she said. "I'm Mrs. Freeley."

I made a loud gulping sound. Some kids heard it and laughed. And there went my face, turning red again.

Mrs. Freeley walked to her desk. She picked up

some papers. Her eyes scanned them quickly. "What's your name?"

"Artie Howard."

"You're not in my class, Artie," she said.

Why did everyone have to stare at me like that?

Okay, I made an honest mistake. I'm the new kid. Can't they cut me some slack?

"What room are you supposed to be in?" Mrs. Freeley asked.

"307," I said.

"This is 307-A," she told me. She pointed. "You're right across the hall."

"Sorry," I said. I grabbed up my backpack and started to the door.

But Brick grabbed my arm. "Stop," he said.

I turned. "What's wrong?"

"You're taking my backpack."

I glanced down. We had the same backpack. I was taking his.

I apologized and made the switch. He just stared at me. Locked his eyes on me with a hard cold look on his face.

I kind of figured he didn't like me.

You probably think my first day at Aardvark wasn't going too well.

Well, don't worry. It'll get worse. Much worse.

9

Across the hall in Room 307, Ms. McVie checked her class list.

She was young and tall with brown hair tied behind her head in a ponytail and dark eyes behind big, round red-plastic eyeglasses.

She wore faded jeans and a brown suede vest over a white sweater. When she spoke, I saw that she had red-and-blue braces on her teeth.

"Artie, why don't you take that seat by the window?" she said, pointing. Then she turned to the class. "Everyone, this is a new student. Artie Howard. I'm sure you'll make him feel at home here at Ardmore."

Silence. Everyone stared at me without a word.

I saw Shelly in the first row. She was the only one who smiled at me.

"Artie, what happened to your hair?" Ms. McVie asked. "Did a bird drop a little something on your head?"

"Uh . . . no. I had a syrup accident," I said.

Thanks a lot, Ms. McVie. Now everyone is staring at my hair.

As I took my seat, I thought about how hot-looking Shelly was. I wondered if she smiled because she liked me.

I dropped the backpack to the floor and stretched my arms above my head. I took a deep breath. The window was wide open, and a sweet-smelling breeze fluttered over me.

It felt good to be in the right place. In the right room with the right teacher and awesome Shelly in the front row.

Ms. McVie sat on the edge of her desk. She crossed her long legs. She started to tell us about what we were going to study this year.

"I guess you're all wondering about that creature," she said. She pointed.

I gasped. Why was she pointing at *me*? Why did she call me a *creature*?

Then I realized she was pointing to the glass case on the window ledge next to me. I gazed inside it and saw a brownish lobstery thing clawing at the glass.

"Not too many sixth-grade classes have a class scorpion," Ms. McVie said. "This is a very rare and valuable scorpion. It comes all the way from the African desert. And I think you will enjoy learning about it this semester."

The scorpion tapped the glass with its claw. Like it was trying to get my attention.

I didn't really like sitting that close to it. What if the lid came off?

"Ms. McVie, will that scorpion sting us?" a girl behind me asked.

I didn't hear the teacher's answer. Because I heard a loud buzzing sound from the open window.

I turned—and a fat bumblebee floated in front of my face. Then the buzz grew louder as it *darted* at me.

I tried to duck. Too late.

I felt bee fur brush my neck as the bee dove down the back of my shirt.

"Yowwwww!" I couldn't help it. I let out a scream.

The bee bumped against my back. My skin prickled.

I leaped to my feet. My arms shot out—

—and my hand hit the glass case on the window ledge. The lid flew off.

"Oh, noooo."

I watched helplessly as . . . as . . . as the rare and valuable scorpion *sailed* out the window.

I made a wild grab for it. Too late.

It was gone.

The bee buzzed against my back. I kicked and squirmed and thrashed around, trying to keep it from stinging me. Trying to force it out from under my T-shirt.

I twisted my body hard—and my desk crashed to the floor.

I guess the deafening crash startled Ms. McVie. Because she fell off the edge of her desk and landed on her butt on the floor with a sharp squeal.

She sat there with a stunned look on her face. Kids jumped up to help her.

I heard a lot of shouting and cries of surprise. I saw Shelly staring at me wide-eyed as I thrashed on my back on the floor.

When the bee finally stung me, I was too exhausted to care.

10

Ms. McVie sent me to the nurse's office. She pulled the bee stinger out of my back. That didn't exactly feel good.

"You've got a nasty bump there," the nurse said. "Let me know if it swells up a lot more. I may have to drain it."

"Sure thing," I said.

I hurried back to the classroom. Ms. McVie was sitting on a pillow on her desk chair. She didn't exactly give me a warm greeting. "You're back?" she said.

I nodded.

"The scorpion must have survived its fall," she told me. "Because we can't find it anywhere. It's probably crawling around somewhere on the playground."

"That's good," I said. I didn't know what else to say.

"I hope no one steps on it," Ms. McVie said. "You know, one sting from that type of scorpion can *kill* a person instantly."

I started to choke.

"Just kidding!" she said. She laughed. "I know. I have a sick sense of humor. Teachers have to make jokes sometimes, Artie. Otherwise . . ." She didn't finish her sentence.

I started to walk to my seat. But she called me back.

"I don't have enough science textbooks," she said. "I need you to go down to the book room and bring up three or four."

"The book room?" My mind started to spin. Another chance to get lost in this huge school building.

"It's in Level Two," she said. "The basement. Mr. Blister will know which books you need. Hurry back."

"Mr. Blister?" I said.

She waved me to the door with both hands.

I trotted out into the hall. I glanced up and down. The long hallway was empty except for one kid. He was struggling to get his locker open. He let out an angry groan and started to kick the locker door with all his might.

Way to lose it, dude.

I turned and walked the other way. Why did the hall smell so sweaty? It was only the first day of school.

The stairs were at the end of the hall. I slid my hand along the metal handrail and hurried down to the first floor.

I could smell food cooking. I guessed the lunchroom was somewhere nearby.

I heard a woman singing scales in a high, shrill voice. "Fa So La Ti Do . . ." Was it the music teacher doing her warm-ups?

An arrow sign read, SECOND LEVEL. So I followed the stairs down one more flight to the basement. The lights were dimmer down here. The tile walls were faded and dirt-smeared.

Water pipes ran along the ceiling. Some of them were draped with cobwebs. The floor was concrete with long cracks and chunks missing.

I shivered. It had to be twenty degrees cooler down here. I thought maybe I could see my breath, but I couldn't.

"Anyone down here?" I called. My voice sounded tiny as it echoed off the low ceiling and walls.

No reply.

Squinting in the dim light, I started down the hall. I passed the furnace room. Empty and silent. Air pipes twisted like snakes in all directions.

The furnace had an enormous black stain down one side. I stopped and gazed at it because it was shaped like a person, arms and legs spread over the furnace wall.

I walked past several closed doors. I glanced down. My sneakers were covered with dust. Didn't anyone ever sweep this basement?

"Hello?—" I called.

Silence.

I ducked under a thick blanket of cobwebs. I grabbed the pipe overhead to keep myself up.

And let out a scream of pain. *"Yowwwwwww!"*

It was a steam pipe—burning hot. I shook my hand hard, trying to shake away the pain.

I opened it and gazed at my palm. An angry red line was burned into my hand.

This is kind of like a horror movie, I thought. *One frightening thing after another.*

That's when I heard the weird moaning sound.

"Whooooaaaaa."

It sounded like a woman. In pain, maybe.

My heart skipped a beat. "Who's there?" I choked out.

"Whoooaaaa."

I saw a half-open door. I peered inside. Total darkness.

"Anyone in here?"

Silence now.

Then I heard a man groan behind me. So close it made me spin around.

No one there.

But how could that be? I heard it so clearly.

I heard the groan again, this time from farther up the hall. And then another long moan.

I felt a chill at the back of my neck. I gasped.

"Oohhhhhhhh."

The frightening moans and groans were all around me. The sounds surrounded me. But I couldn't see anyone there.

Keep moving, Artie, I thought.

I lowered my head like a football running back and charged down the hall. My sneakers kicked up dust as I turned a corner and started down another endless, dimly lit hall.

"Mr. Blister? Are you down here?"

My voice came out weak and muffled. I tried again, cupping my hands around my mouth. "Mr. Blister?"

Was that really his name? Where was the book room?

Yellow-gray light poured out from an open doorway. I stopped to peer inside the room.

It took a few seconds for my eyes to adjust. I saw a table. A long metal table. And a man . . .

Huh?

A man lying on the table. A blanket draped over him. Like an operating table you see in all the hospital shows.

A man lying on his back. His arms dangled off the sides of the table. He didn't move.

A corpse?

A dead man lying in the basement of the school?

"No! That's *impossible*!" I cried out loud.

And then someone grabbed me—gripped my shoulder hard from behind.

And I opened my mouth in a shriek of horror.

11

The grip tightened on my shoulder. I felt hot breath on the back of my neck.

I spun around—and saw a huge fat man standing behind me. His enormous, hairy stomach bulged down to his knees. His sweatshirt only covered a tiny part of it.

He was almost as wide as the hallway. I'm not exaggerating. And so tall, he had to duck his head under the ceiling pipes.

He was bald and pink-skinned. He had pointed ears like a *Star Trek* character. One brown eye and one blue eye. His face had so many chins, it looked like a candle melting onto his shirt.

"Sorry if I startled you. Are you looking for me?" His voice was soft and distant. As if it were coming from deep in his huge belly.

His stomach rumbled. It sounded like the ocean crashing onto a beach.

His stomach was, like, alive. A big living creature. I suddenly remembered a gigantic stuffed walrus I saw at the Natural History Museum.

"Are you—are you Mr. Blister?" I stuttered.

He nodded. All of his chins moved.

He clenched and unclenched his fists. His hands were pink and meaty. His fingers looked like little salamis.

"You need books?" he asked.

I nodded.

Under his sweatshirt, his stomach bobbed up and down like an enormous beach ball. "Follow me. What's your name?"

"Artie Howard," I said.

"A new kid," he muttered. He heaved himself forward.

That's the only way I can say it. He didn't walk. He was too fat to walk. He *heaved* himself.

It was like those big steamrollers you see rumbling down the street. Only, Mr. Blister rocked from side to side as he rolled forward.

His big body bumped and scraped the walls as he moved down the hall. His stomach rumbled again. It really sounded like the ocean tide rushing in.

What does this guy eat for lunch?

I tried not to think about it as I followed him to the end of the hall. He led me into a big room with bookshelves on all four walls. The shelves were filled with textbooks from floor to ceiling.

"This is my book room," Blister announced, waving his fat arms.

Light poured over us from a big ceiling fixture. Rows of bookshelves filled the middle of the room.

He led me to a wall of TV monitors. Carefully, he lowered himself into a low chair in front of the monitors.

As I came closer, I saw that the monitors showed classrooms. A different class on each screen.

Did this school have video cameras in every classroom? Why was he down here watching them?

I had a dozen questions I wanted to ask the man. But the question that I blurted out was the one that scared me the most. "Did I see a dead body back there?" I asked him.

He blinked his eyes. He rubbed a few of his chins. "No, you didn't," he said.

"On that table," I said. "I saw a man under a blanket."

"No, you didn't," he said.

"The man was on his back. He didn't move," I said. "I saw him—"

"No, you didn't," Blister said. "Why would you see something like that in a normal, average middle school?"

"But—"

"It just wouldn't happen," he said. He stared at me with his two-colored eyes. Stared hard, as if challenging me to argue with him. "You probably saw a pile of dust."

"Excuse me? Dust?"

"It's very dusty down here," Blister said. "Herbert, the janitor, won't come down here and sweep. He refuses to work in the basement."

"Why?" I asked.

"He thinks the basement is *haunted,*" Blister said. Then he burst out laughing. He had a weird laugh. It sounded more like swallowing.

"What book do you need?" he asked finally.

"Science book," I said. "For sixth grade. Ms. McVie's class. I need three or four."

"No problem," Blister muttered.

He opened a drawer under the monitors and pulled something out. A tape measure. He squeezed it in his meaty hand. "Come closer, Artie."

I stepped closer. He heaved himself to his feet

with a loud groan. His stomach nearly bounced on the floor. He pulled the sweatshirt halfway down over it.

Then he wrapped the tape around my waist and measured me. "Twenty-six."

Before I could move away, he raised the tape and wrapped it around my forehead. Squinting, he read off the numbers. Then he squatted over his table and wrote them down.

"Whoa. I don't get it," I said. "What are you doing?"

"You have to be measured for books," he said. He wrapped the tape around my right arm and checked the number.

"Why?" I demanded. "What's up with this? Why do I have to be measured to get a textbook?"

"School rule," he said. He sighed. "Turn around."

"But—but—" I sputtered.

I felt him push the tape against my back. "Forty-one," he murmured.

"They didn't measure us at my old school," I said.

He mumbled something into his chins.

And then I felt a sharp stab of pain.

I let out a shocked cry. "Hey—why'd you *do* that?"

Blister had pulled out a few strands of hair from the back of my head. My scalp still hurt.

He stood there holding the hair between his

thumb and finger. Then he tucked the hair into an envelope and slid it into the drawer next to the tape measure.

"Why'd you do that?" I repeated.

"School rule," he said. "School rule."

12

I was so happy to get out of that basement. I ran all the way back to Ms. McVie's class, holding the four heavy textbooks in my arms.

The rest of the morning, I kept thinking about Mr. Blister and everything I had seen down there. It was all strange and frightening—not like a normal school basement.

I tried to shut it all out of my mind and listen to what Ms. McVie was saying. But I kept picturing that big blob of a man in front of his TV monitors. Pictured him measuring me so carefully and ripping out some of my hair.

What was *that* about?

Anyway, I was happy to sit at my desk and feel the nice breeze from outside. I had no more disasters. Until lunchtime, that is.

Of course, I dropped my food tray in the lunchroom.

Someone has to drop their food tray, right? And then everyone laughs and bursts into wild applause.

Well, here I was, the new kid on his first day of school. And it had to be me.

I loaded up my tray. I was starving. I took a big bowl of spaghetti and one of those small, round pizzas and some big pretzel sticks and some kind of pudding dessert.

And then I turned to find a place to sit—and slipped on something wet on the lunchroom floor. And, you can picture it. I don't really need to describe it to you because you see it all the time.

I stumbled. The tray went flying. Somehow the food all tipped over in the air.

The spaghetti made a wet *smack* as it hit the floor. The pudding bowl broke and shattered. Pretzels rolled in every direction.

Kids laughed and clapped and pointed at me.

"Smooth move!"

"Nice catch!"

"Do it again!"

One more chance for my face to turn bright red.

What next? I thought. I spun away from the cheering kids—and there was Shelly.

She wasn't laughing at me. "Let me help you," she said.

We both bent down to start picking up the spilled food—and we cracked heads.

"Owww!" Shelly howled. She stumbled back and raised her hand to her forehead.

I shook my head, dazed. *I can't believe I just did that.*

A teacher walked by and examined Shelly's forehead. "You're going to have a nasty bump there," she said. "Better put some ice on it."

"That's okay," Shelly said. She raised her eyes to me. "You okay, Artie?"

I nodded. "You're being nice to me because I'm the new kid—aren't you," I said.

"Yes," she said. She told me to go fill up another food tray. She said I could come sit with her at her table.

I couldn't believe she was being so kind. I started back to the food line. But I stepped in the pile of fallen spaghetti on the floor. My feet went flying—and I landed on my butt in the spaghetti.

Again, wild laughter rocked the room.

"Do that again!"

"Awesome!"

"That kid is *smooth*!"

I knew my face was beet red. Brushing the spaghetti noodles off the seat of my jeans, I slumped back to the lunch line.

A few minutes later, I sat down across from her at a table near the front of the room. She was spooning blueberry yogurt into her mouth. She smiled at me.

Some kids in the back were having a milk-carton fight. They splashed milk on each other, then heaved the cartons at each other's faces.

I chose a peanut-butter sandwich this time. Much safer.

"You just move here?" Shelly asked.

I nodded. "Yeah." I chewed my sandwich.

"First day in a new school is the pits," she said.

I nodded. "Yeah. The pits."

I couldn't believe I was sitting and talking with the most beautiful girl in school. Sure, a few unlucky, painful things had happened to me. But watching Shelly spoon her yogurt, I knew this had to be an *awesome* day.

Too bad that was the end of our talk.

Brick dropped his backpack to the floor and sank his big body into the seat next to Shelly. "Hey, whussup? How's it going?" he asked her.

He spread his lunch out on the table. I counted

three pizzas, two bowls of spaghetti, four pudding bowls, three apples, and a bunch of bananas.

"You on a diet?" I said.

He ignored me. He leaned all over Shelly as he stuffed food into his mouth. The two of them talked about the football team and how great he was.

"You ever try a peanut-butter-and-banana sandwich?" I asked.

They just kept on talking. He scooted one of his pudding bowls over to her, and they shared it.

"I like it when they put the chocolate and the vanilla together," I said.

I didn't exist. I was invisible.

They kept yakking away. They gossiped about the girls at the next table. Then Shelly told Brick how Ms. McVie had fallen off her desk.

They both laughed.

"Hey—I'm the one who made her fall!" I exclaimed.

They didn't even look at me.

I jammed the rest of the sandwich into my mouth. Then I jumped up. I knew when I wasn't wanted.

They were both talking and laughing. They didn't even notice that I was leaving. I picked up my backpack and headed out of the lunchroom.

Was I unhappy? Does peanut butter stick to the roof of your mouth like cement?

Yes, I felt totally rejected. Shelly and I were having such a nice talk—until Brick barged in.

A bell rang, jarring me from my bitter thoughts. It was the warning bell. It meant five more minutes until class.

I shifted the backpack on my shoulders. I was still working my tongue against the roof of my mouth, trying to scrape off the peanut butter.

I saw the boys' room across the hall. I pulled open the door and stepped inside.

The lights were so bright, it took a few seconds for my eyes to adjust.

And then the screams began.

And a girl popped her head out from a stall. "You creep!" she cried. "You *creep*! What are you doing in the girls' room?"

13

"Uh . . . sorry," I muttered.

Another girl heaved a roll of toilet paper. It bounced off my forehead.

"Sorry." I backed out the door—right into Mr. Jenks.

The principal uttered a cry as my heel stomped down on his foot. "Artie?"

I caught my balance and whirled around to face him. He was still wearing the suit jacket with the pocket ripped off.

"Artie," he said, "did I just see you come out of the girls' bathroom?"

"Uh . . . yeah," I said.

He rested a hand on my shoulder and leaned his face close. "Do we need to have a talk?" he said softly.

"I . . . don't . . . think . . . so," I replied.

He squeezed my shoulder. Then he rubbed the spot on his jacket where his pocket used to be.

"Well, let's just review, shall we?" he said. "You brought your dog to school, and he ripped my new suit. You tossed a valuable scorpion out the second-floor window. And now I see you coming out of the girls' bathroom."

"I didn't toss the scorpion," I said. "I bumped it, and it *fell* out the window."

He stared at me for a long time. "Be careful, Artie. One more incident," he said finally. "One more strike, and you're out."

"Out?" I said. My voice cracked.

"Out," he repeated.

"Okay. No problem," I said.

The second bell rang. That meant I was late for class. I hurried up the stairs and took off running. My sneakers slapped loudly in the empty hallway.

I burst breathlessly into Ms. McVie's class. She had her back turned. She was scribbling math problems on the whiteboard.

The other kids were already writing down the problem. Shelly didn't look up as I sneaked past her to my seat.

I slid in behind the desk. Then I opened the

backpack to get a writing pad. I reached inside—and pulled out something odd.

A jockstrap!

Startled, I raised it in front of me. "Hey!" I cried. "This isn't mine!"

Kids started to laugh.

Ms. McVie spun around to see what the fuss was about.

"This isn't mine!" I cried, holding the jockstrap up in front of me.

Kids laughed harder.

Ms. McVie's eyes bulged. "Artie?—Why did you bring that thing to class?"

"It isn't mine," I repeated.

Suddenly, I knew what I had done. I'd picked up Brick's backpack from the lunchroom by mistake.

And then, there he was. There was Brick. Standing beside my desk. Scowling angrily at me as I held his jockstrap in the air.

He made a grab for it and pulled it from my hand.

"Dude," he whispered, "you're in a world of trouble."

14

Could I think about math problems after that?

Actually, my hand was shaking so hard, I couldn't even write them down.

Brick grabbed his backpack and hurried to his own class. But his threat lingered in my mind. And those dreaded words—*you're in a world of trouble*—drowned out everything Ms. McVie said.

What exactly was he planning for me?

He was the most popular guy in school. Everyone liked him. So he couldn't really be a thug—could he? He didn't go around punching out your lights just because you made a little backpack mistake.

Or did he?

I couldn't hear Ms. McVie. I couldn't hear anyone else in the room. I couldn't think about anything else.

And when the teacher announced a fifteen-minute

break—time for us to go hang outside for some fresh air—I didn't want to leave my seat. I wanted to stay in the safety of the classroom.

The other kids jumped up, eager to leave.

"Ms. McVie," I called, "I think I'll just sit here and get fresh air from the window."

She shook her head no. She waved me to the door.

I had no choice. I had to go outside.

Brick won't be waiting for me out in the hall, I told myself. *Brick will be hanging out with his friends. He probably forgot the whole jockstrap thing already.*

But, a bad day only gets worse.

I took three steps out of the classroom—and there he was.

Brick stood across the hall with a scowl on his face. He was waiting with a friend, a black dude who was just as big and powerful-looking as Brick. The friend scowled, too.

"Come over here, Artie," Brick said. Not in a friendly way. Not like, *"Come over here and let's chat."*

"Darnell and I have been waiting for you," Brick said.

Darnell waved a big fist in the air.

Do you think he was sending a message?

"Well, you'll have to wait a while longer," I said. And I took off.

I lowered my head and shoulders and ran through the hall like a running back. The hallway was jammed with kids on their break. Kids at their lockers. Kids in groups of twos and threes, making their way out to the playground.

I ducked my head and shoved between two teachers. They shouted for me to stop.

No way.

I glanced back. Brick and Darnell were coming after me. They looked like two angry bulls stampeding after a matador.

I jumped over a kid who was down on the floor tying his shoe. I danced between a group of girls. They scattered as I burst through.

"Yo! Artie! Wait!" Brick shouted.

They were gaining on me. Just a few feet behind me. They had their arms outstretched to grab me.

I was nearly to the stairs. But I knew I couldn't escape them.

Stop running, Artie, I told myself. *They can't hurt you too bad inside school. They don't want to get in trouble.*

So I reached the top of the stairs, and I stopped.

Something bumped my ankle and almost knocked me over.

It took me a few seconds to realize it was Brick.

Brick tripped over my ankle. His arms shot out as he sailed into the air. And I gasped in horror as he went tumbling down the stairs.

Thud thud thud thud.

His head banged the concrete steps. It hit every step as he rolled over and over all the way down to the bottom.

He screamed all the way.

Then . . . silence.

A terrifying silence.

I stood at the top of the stairwell, my whole body shaking.

Darnell was frozen on the top step. He stood stiffly, arms at his sides, mouth open. His dark eyes were wide with fright and shock.

And then a girl's scream rang out from the bottom of the stairs.

"You killed him!" she cried up at me. "You KILLED him!"

15

I opened my mouth in a scream, but no sound came out.

Darnell stood next to me, a statue, frozen in horror. "Oh, no. No way," he murmured.

I forced myself to move and went tearing down the stairs.

Kids shrieked and screamed.

I saw Brick sprawled on the floor on his back. His eyes were closed. One leg split out from his body in a weird position.

Slowly, he raised his head and groaned. "Give me a break," he choked out. "I'm not dead."

The screams and cries stopped. A hush fell over the hallway.

Brick uttered a cry of pain. He twisted his face in a grimace. "My leg . . . ," he moaned.

Two teachers came running up. One of them, a tall, skinny young man in jeans and a smiley-face T-shirt, motioned for the crowd of kids to step back.

The other teacher, an older guy with short, gray hair and a gray beard, dropped down beside Brick. "His leg is badly broken," he said. "Don't anybody move him."

"My leg?—" Brick groaned.

"It's fractured in at least two places," the teacher said. "Don't look at it. It's not pretty."

"But the football team—" Brick started.

The teacher shook his head. "Your season is over, Brick."

Suddenly, I realized everyone was looking at *me*.

As soon as the teacher told Brick, "Your season is over," everyone turned their accusing eyes on me.

Before I could get away from there, Darnell stepped up close. He pressed his mouth to my ear, and he whispered, "I'm going to get you after school, punk face."

Punk face?

I swallowed hard. I had a heavy feeling in the pit of my stomach.

Would everyone in the school *hate* me now?

16

"Everyone in the school hates you now," Mr. Jenks said. "But you shouldn't take it personally, Artie."

Mr. Jenks called me out of class as soon as the paramedics left and the ambulance carrying Brick rolled away with its siren blaring. Now I sat in a little folding chair in his office while he paced back and forth behind his desk.

His usual cheerful face had vanished. That smile that was always there—guess what? It wasn't there.

This is the worst day of my life, I told myself. *My first day in this school and every single student already hates me. That's hard to do in one day.*

"I know it's unusual for a middle school," Jenks continued. "But we take our football program very seriously. Brick is known all over the state. He was our hope for the new season."

He stopped pacing. He drilled his gaze into me. “And now that hope is smashed. Broken. Broken in several places.”

I lowered my eyes to the floor. I clasped my hands tightly in my lap. I didn’t know what to say.

“I know it was an accident,” Mr. Jenks said. “You didn’t shove Brick down a flight of stairs. Of course, it was an accident.”

“Yes, it was,” I murmured, keeping my head down.

“I understand you almost sent Ms. McVie to the hospital, too,” he said. “You made her fall off her desk?”

“Also . . . an accident,” I stammered.

“But, Artie,” he continued in his soft, feathery voice. “Artie, you have to ask yourself why so many accidents happen wherever you go.”

“Yes,” I said. I didn’t know what I was supposed to say. I just wanted to get out of his office.

No. Actually, I wanted to get out of this school and never come back.

Maybe—if I asked him nicely—he would throw me out of school?

“One more thing,” Jenks said. He sat down behind his cluttered desk. He tapped the desk with both hands. He rubbed his bald head.

"I asked Darnell and some of his teammates to beat you up after school," the principal said.

My mouth dropped open. I didn't mean to, but I made a sick gagging sound.

"You *what*?" I finally choked out. My voice was too high for dogs to hear.

Jenks tapped his fingers on the desk. "I asked some of Brick's friends on the football team to beat you up after school," he said.

"But—but—" I sputtered.

"I asked them to give you a really good pounding on behalf of Brick and everyone here at Ardmore Middle School," Jenks said.

My chest felt fluttery. I had that heavy feeling in my stomach again. I jumped to my feet.

"But you're a school principal," I said. "You can't *do* that!"

Jenks frowned at me. "Artie, I have to do what I think is fair," he said.

17

I wanted the rest of the afternoon to drag on forever. I didn't want the final bell to ring. I knew it would be the final bell for *me.*

But the afternoon seemed to fly by in five minutes flat.

When the bell rang, I jumped to my feet. My legs felt shaky. My throat was too dry to swallow. My eyes darted from side to side, as if I expected Darnell and his buddies to jump me right in the classroom.

I hurried to the door, but Shelly stepped in front of me. "Did anyone warn you?" she asked in a whisper.

"Yes," I said. "I—"

"Did they tell you the football team plans to punch your lights out as soon as you step out of the building?"

"Yes," I said. "They told me."

"Okay," she said. "Just wondered." Then she added, "It's nothing personal, Artie. I mean, Darnell and the other guys are really the nicest kids in the school. They never get into fights or anything."

"Could I walk out with you?" I asked. My voice cracked. "Maybe if you and I are walking together, they won't want to punch me into orange-juice pulp."

"I wish I could," Shelly said. "But I have a tennis lesson."

She gave me a little wave and hurried out the door.

She's so totally nice, I told myself. *She really wanted to help me.*

I was wasting time. I knew what I had to do. Get to my locker. Dump all my stuff. Sneak out through a back door and run home.

I had to be fast. The football players might already be ready and waiting for me. Maybe waiting by the front door. Maybe waiting down on the street.

I kept my eyes alert as I trotted down the hall along the row of lockers. I stopped in front of mine and dropped my backpack to the floor.

My hand was shaking so hard, I could barely grip the combination lock.

The hall was still crowded with kids. I kept

glancing behind me, expecting to see the angry football players swarming in on me.

I checked the back of my hand. That's where I wrote the lock combination this morning so I wouldn't forget it: "30" to the right. "12" to the left. "00" to the right.

I heard footsteps. Heavy running footsteps.

I gasped. Turned around.

No. A bunch of kids hurried past without looking at me.

I turned back to the lock. I held it with both hands to stop it from shaking.

30-12-00.

I tugged on the lock.

No. It didn't budge.

Did I do something wrong?

I checked the black Sharpie writing on my hand. "30-12-00."

I had it right. I must have turned it wrong.

I glanced all around. No sign of my punishers.

I took a deep breath. Began to twirl the lock dial again. Carefully . . . very carefully.

I tugged it down. No. The lock didn't spring open.

"Come on! Come on! *Open!*" I shouted angrily. I kicked the locker.

I was frantic. I had to get away from here before they found me.

I grabbed the side of the locker door with both hands and tried to pull it open. No.

I tried to slide my fingers under the metal door and pry it open.

I was straining my muscles, pulling on the door with all my strength when I felt a tap on my shoulder.

I gasped. And spun around. And stared at Darnell, breathing hard over me.

"Dude, what's up with you? Now you're breaking into my locker?" he said. "Is there something you want in there?"

18

I made a gulping sound. I pulled my hands from the locker door and glanced at the number near the top.

Oops. Wrong locker.

"My bad," I said. I backed away. "My locker is over there. Sorry. You know. First day of school."

I could tell from the deep scowl on Darnell's face that he didn't accept my apology. He began to breathe harder, his big chest heaving up and down beneath his T-shirt.

He was about to pounce.

Down the hall, I saw a bunch of other boys with hard expressions on their faces. They were moving toward me with their hands clenched into fists. Somehow I could tell they weren't coming to welcome me to my new school.

Time to run away.

I didn't wait. I moved like a running back. I took a few running steps right at them. Just to fake them out.

Then I made a sharp swerve, spun around, and took off down the hall in the other direction.

My move didn't fool them at all. Darnell led the way as they came thundering after me. It sounded like a cattle stampede in one of those old movies.

Kids leaped out of the way. The football players lowered their heads and ran like . . . like football players.

I whipped around a corner. I was looking for a door, a way out. Maybe if I made it outside, I could hide behind some parents who had come to pick up their kids.

But this hallway just led to another hallway. Gasping for breath, I tried to run harder. But my side started to ache. My leg muscles began to throb.

The team members were close behind, shouting as they ran:

"Hey, dead meat—"

"Don't run away. Be a man!"

"We won't hurt you *too* much!"

"Dead Meat! You know your name? It's Dead Meat!"

Very clever.

I knew I couldn't run much further. I spun around another corner—and spotted an open locker.

I didn't have to think about it. I dove into the locker and pulled the door shut.

Did they see me? Had I put myself in a trap?

My heart pounded so hard, my chest ached. I held my breath. I listened.

They thundered right past the locker and kept going.

I could hear them roaring down the hall. I waited a few seconds. Then I popped open the locker door and jumped out. I darted in the other direction, searching for a way out.

I knew in a few seconds they'd turn around and come back after me.

When I saw the stairs leading down to the basement, I screeched to a stop. Could I lose them down there?

There were definitely more places to hide in that dark, creepy basement, I decided. I grabbed the railing and dove down the stairs two at a time.

I found myself back in the dusty, dimly lit, cobwebbed hall. Ducking under the fat pipes overhead, I made my way past closed doors.

My shoes kicked up the thick layer of dust on the concrete floor. I heard machinery humming, water flowing through pipes, strange squeaks and squeals.

I listened for the shouts and heavy, galloping

footsteps of the football team. Had they figured out that I was down here?

Yes. I heard shouts far behind me. Getting louder.

Where should I hide?

Shadows reached out as if to grab me. A fat spider dangled in front of my face. I brushed it away as I studied the long hall.

Most of the doors were closed. I passed a small supply closet filled with buckets and dried-up mops. No room for me in there.

I peered into the next room. Too dark to see anything.

"Ooooohhhh." Was that a low groan from the back of the room? Was someone in there?

I fought back my fear. Tried to slow my thundering heartbeats.

I had to keep moving. I started to jog, brushing away cobwebs as I ran.

I didn't stop till I reached the book room. I stepped inside, breathing hard. I glanced at the stack of monitors against the wall. They all showed empty classrooms.

No sign of Mr. Blister.

I gazed around the room. Books were stacked from the floor to the ceiling.

I decided I could hide back in the bookshelves.

The tall shelves rose up like dark walls. A perfect place to lose my pursuers.

I slipped between two rows of shelves and made my way to the back wall. The shelves blocked out all light. It was hot back here. It smelled of old dust and decay.

I heard shouts out in the hall. The football players were coming close to the book room.

I started to hunch down against one of the shelves. But then I glimpsed an open doorway in the back wall.

What was back there?

My heart pounding, I crept along the shelf, then darted into the room. I pulled the door shut behind me.

Total blackness.

My hand fumbled against the wall till I found a light switch. I clicked it, and a ceiling light flashed on. Blinking, I waited for my eyes to adjust.

I was in a long, narrow room. The floor was black. So were the walls.

"Hey—" I cried out. I wasn't alone. I saw dozens of people jammed into the room. People standing together side by side in rows of four. Some standing on low metal tables.

It took only a few seconds to realize they weren't

moving. They weren't alive. Were they mannequins?

They were wrapped in some kind of gauze. Like mummies. Four long rows of human-size mannequins. Their heads and bodies were hidden under thick layers of gauze.

I swallowed hard. My throat suddenly felt dry. I felt a stab of fear in my chest.

What *were* they? Why were they hidden down here in the basement of the school?

I took a step closer. I reached out a hand. I touched the head of the nearest figure.

And it *spoke.*

"I'm Artie," it said in a tinny voice. *My* voice!

"I'm Artie. I'm Artie. I'm Artie."

"Noooooo!" I opened my mouth in a scream of horror.

I fell back . . .

. . . fell back . . .

. . . and woke up in my bed. Still screaming. Woke up in my bed, shrieking my lungs out. Back in my room. Under the covers in my own bed.

Was the whole school day a dream? *Was* it?

DAY ONE

1

I stopped screaming a few seconds before the alarm went off.

The loud buzz startled me, and I fell out of bed. I landed hard on the wood floor. My head hit the floor and bounced once or twice. I actually saw stars, just like in the cartoons.

I tried to blink away the pain that throbbed through my head. And tried to make the room stop spinning.

Before I could pull myself up, Mom walked into my room.

"Artie, what are you doing down on the floor?"

"I can't believe it," I muttered. "How could I fall out of bed two mornings in a row?"

Mom stared hard at me.

"And I hit my head again," I said.

She walked over and helped pull me to my feet. "You're just nervous about your first day of school," she said.

"Huh?" I tugged down my pajama shirt and squinted at her. "First day? Did you forget yesterday?"

"What was yesterday?" Mom asked. "Sunday. What about Sunday?"

"Yesterday was the first day of school," I insisted.

She rubbed my hair. "Artie, I think you hit your head really hard. You *know* that today is the first day of school."

She picked up a pile of dirty clothes I'd tossed on the floor. "Now hurry up and get dressed. Your brother is already downstairs. I'm making waffles."

I watched her carry the clothes out of my room.

"We had waffles yesterday morning," I said to myself. I reached up and felt the side of my hair. Not sticky.

I stood there without moving for a long moment. Trying to get my thoughts together. So . . . my first day at Aardvark Middle School had all been a dream. A nightmare because I was stressed about starting a new school.

It had all seemed so real. So *painfully* real.

But today was the actual first day of school.

How did that make me feel?

Awesome!

That had been the worst, most frightening, most horrifying day of my life. And it hadn't happened. None of it was real.

"Yaaaaaay!" I let out a happy cheer. I did a crazy dance around my room.

I was getting a fresh start. A whole new beginning to my school year.

What to wear on the first day? I'd spent hours thinking about it. But I just couldn't decide.

Two days before, I spread all my T-shirts out on the bed. Which was the coolest? None of them? I definitely needed new T-shirts.

Finally, I picked the black T-shirt that just said T-SHIRT across the front. It was pretty funny, I thought. I pulled it down over my jeans.

I picked up my phone. The little battery up in the corner was blinking. No power. But didn't I just power it up yesterday?

I guessed I was still mixed up because of that very real dream.

Oh, well. Plenty of time to power it up while I was having breakfast.

I found the charger. Stuck it into the phone. Then

I jammed the plug into the outlet near my floor. And . . .

ZZZZZZZZZZAAAAAAAP.

Electricity jolted through my body. I did a wild dance around my room. My arms thrashed the air, out of control.

Didn't the same thing happen in my dream?

I could still feel the current rushing through me as I hurried down to the kitchen for breakfast. Dad had already left for work. Mom was pouring herself a cup of coffee.

Wowser was at his usual place beneath the table. He spent his whole life waiting for someone to drop some food on the floor.

My five-year-old brother Eddy was already at the table, digging his fork deep into a stack of syrup-covered toaster waffles.

"Morning, Piggy," I said.

He burped in reply. Eddy has one major talent. He can burp whenever he wants to. And his burps are totally wet and disgusting.

"Waffles again?" I said to Mom.

She squinted at me as she took a sip from her coffee mug. "Again? What do you mean?"

"Didn't we have them yesterday?"

Eddy laughed. "We had cereal. Remember? I spilled my milk?"

"We haven't had toaster waffles in weeks," Mom said.

"Oh. Right," I replied.

I sat down across from Eddy. He swung his hand and knocked over his orange-juice glass. A river of orange juice came washing over to my side.

I jumped up. I'd almost gotten orange-juice stains on my jeans.

Eddy laughed. Then he burped again.

I rolled my eyes. "You are so not funny."

Mom wiped up the orange juice. "Artie, don't forget your dentist appointment after school," she said. "Bring your cell phone. Take the bus to the dentist and call me when you get there."

The toaster at the end of the table popped. I grabbed two waffles and dropped them onto my plate. They burned my fingers. But they smelled so good!

I reached for the syrup bottle. Eddy reached for it at the same time. "More syrup," he grunted.

He squeezed the bottle. Thick brown syrup sprayed up from the bottle.

"Oh, noooo!" I uttered a cry. I tried to duck away.

But a thick glob of syrup landed in my hair.

"This can't be happening!" I shrieked. I jumped away from the table. Too late. I felt the sweet, sticky goo sliding down the side of my head. And I felt it trickle onto the shoulder of my T-shirt.

I reached my hand up and slid it along my hair. Now my hand was sticky and wet, too.

"Mom!" I cried. "Help me! You've *got* to help me!"

"Artie, calm down," she said quietly. "It's only syrup."

"N-no. You don't understand," I stammered. "My dream. The horrible nightmare I had about my first day of school. I think it's *coming* true!"

2

No time to wash my hair. I wanted to stay home. Just skip school. How could I go to a new school with my fat, curly hair standing up on one side and glued flat to my head on the other?

No way.

But Mom said there was no way I was missing the first day because of a little sticky hair.

So I pulled a baseball cap down low on my head, picked up my backpack, took Eddy's hand, and started to take him to his school.

It had rained the night before. Big pools of water and deep puddles marked the street and sidewalks.

As always, Eddy had to jump like a chimpanzee from puddle to puddle. He splashed up tall waves all around him and got himself soaked. But he didn't care. He thought it was funny.

I think he's very immature for a five-year-old. And I'm not saying that just because he's my brother.

I'm saying it because he's a total pain in the butt.

I tried to stay as far away from him as I could. But Mom's rule was that I had to hold his hand when we crossed the street.

We walked the three blocks to his school. He was jumping and splashing and hee-hawing and having a great time. I hoped no one from my school walked by and saw me with him.

That would be totally embarrassing.

I could see the big sign across the street: CYRUS ELEMENTARY, HOME OF THE FIGHTING BUMBLEBEES.

We stepped up to the corner. I looked up and down the street to make sure no cars were coming.

Then I remembered the truck in my dream. The gasoline truck that came roaring by and splashed rainwater in an embarrassing place on my jeans.

Sure, it was a dream. But I had to play it safe. I couldn't let that happen again.

"Let's step back," I told Eddy. I started to pull him away from the corner.

But Eddy stuck his pointer finger out and jabbed it into my stomach. "I'm a bumblebee!" he said. "*Bzzzz. Bzzzz.* I'm a bumblebee."

He jabbed his finger into my stomach again.

"I sting you! I'm a bumblebee."

He tried to sting me again. I jumped to the side—

—just as a long, silver gasoline truck came racing past.

The big tires rolled through a deep puddle—and sent a tall wave of rainwater over the sidewalk.

I felt a splash of cold on the front of my jeans.

I didn't have to look down. I knew exactly what had happened.

Eddy started prancing around. He tossed his head back and let out a crazy, wild laugh.

He pointed at the front of my jeans and shouted, "You look like you peed!"

3

Okay. This was starting to freak me out.

Let's say last night I had a bad dream about my first day of school. And let's say it was a very *real* dream.

There's no way that dream could come true—right?

I mean, step by step? Every detail?

But here I was with a sticky syrup head and wet jeans.

I don't scare easy. I'm the one in my family who goes to scary movies and laughs his head off.

You can leap out of a closet and grab me around the throat. Or climb out from under my bed screaming in the middle of the night. And I won't make a peep.

I just stay cool and calm.

But standing across from Eddy's school, watching

the gasoline truck rumble off into the distance . . . I admit it. I was freaked.

What next?

Well, I took Eddy to his kindergarten class. No problem there. Except that Eddy ran into the room shouting, "My brother peed his pants! My brother peed his pants!"

And all the kids went crazy, staring at me and pointing and laughing like lunatics. That's about as funny as it gets to a five-year-old.

"Thanks, Eddy. I owe you one," I said. And I ran out of his school as fast as I could.

I tried to take my time walking to my school. To give my jeans a chance to dry. But Ardmore Middle School was only two blocks away. The jeans still had that dark stain on the front as I started up the steps.

I climbed a few steps, then stopped. "Whoa."

Freak-out time again. Because the school looked exactly like the school in my dream. A tall, gray stone building with four floors, lots of windows, and a wall of ivy creeping down from the roof.

I felt a chill at the back of my neck.

Yes, I was here with my parents last summer when they enrolled me. I saw the school before. But still . . . it shouldn't match my dream so totally—should it?

I shook off the weird feeling and climbed the rest

of the way up. Other kids ran past. I saw them glancing at my jeans.

Wasn't I tense enough about the first day of school? Did I really need to walk around totally embarrassed?

A bald man in a brown suit was greeting kids at the double entrance doors. I recognized him. Mr. Jenks, the principal.

My parents and I had a nice talk with him last summer. He was a smiley kind of guy. He had twinkly blue eyes and a warm smile that never seemed to leave his face.

He was shaking hands and talking to every kid who came to the door. "Hey, Artie. Hi," he said, shaking my hand. He turned that warm smile on me. I smelled peppermint on his breath.

"Welcome to Ardmore," he said.

Was he staring at the front of my jeans?

Mr. Jenks adjusted the collar of the yellow turtleneck he wore under his suit jacket.

Was that the same color turtleneck he wore in my dream?

"First you need to find whose class you are in," he told me. "The class lists are posted on the wall in front of my office."

"I know," I said.

He squinted at me. "You do?"

Some kids at the bottom of the stairs were tossing a baseball back and forth. The ball got away from one of them and bounced halfway up the steps. A girl picked it up and tossed it back to them.

I started to step past Mr. Jenks into the school. But he put a hand on my shoulder to stop me.

"Artie, I'm sorry. We don't wear baseball caps in this school. Could you please remove yours?"

"Uh . . . okay," I said.

I started to tug the cap off, but it stuck to my syrupy hair. I suddenly remembered why I was wearing it. With my hair half stuck to my head, I looked like a total freak.

"Do you think I could keep it on just for today?" I asked him.

He shook his head. His smile didn't fade. "No. I'm sorry. No exceptions. Take it off."

I pulled the cap off. Some of my hair came off with it.

"Artie." Mr. Jenks leaned close to me and spoke in my ear. "I'm the law around here," he said. "You don't want to fight the law, do you?"

"Law?" I said. I wasn't sure I was hearing him correctly.

"You don't want to fight the law, Artie," Jenks repeated. "Because I could put you in a world of pain."

4

It was noisy out on the steps. I knew I didn't hear what the principal said. He didn't *really* say he could put me in a world of pain.

That would be crazy.

Jenks was still smiling warmly at me. He turned away and started to say hello to twin girls. They had red hair and green eyes and wore matching denim outfits.

I was nearly through the front door when I heard a racket behind me.

Kids shouted.

A dog yapped.

"Huh?" I spun around—and instantly recognized the big dog racing up the steps. "Wowser!"

Oh, no. Wowser had followed me to school.

"Wowser—down!" I shouted.

I couldn't move fast enough. The huge dog leaped onto Mr. Jenks. Wowser pawed the principal's suit, leaving big mud stains on the shoulders and down the front.

Then I heard a loud *Rrrriiip.*

Wowser tore the jacket pocket right off the principal's suit.

"Get down! Get down!" Jenks tried to back away. But he hit the wall. "Artie—is this your dog?"

"Get down, Wowser!" I shouted. "Down, boy!"

Mr. Jenks swatted a hand at the dog's snout, trying to push him back.

Then . . . *crunnnnch.*

A sick *crunch* sound as Wowser snapped his jaws on the principal's hand.

"He bit me! He *bit* me!" Jenks shrieked.

I watched a line of bright red blood spurt up on the back of his hand. Jenks shook the hand. Blood dripped onto his shoes.

I wrapped my arms around Wowser's neck and pulled him away from the principal. "He . . . he never bit anyone before," I stammered. "He's usually very gentle."

"Must have smelled my cat," Jenks said. He cradled his bleeding hand in his good hand.

Kids crowded the entrance, watching in silence.

Down on the sidewalk, the two guys kept throwing their baseball back and forth.

I held Wowser firmly by his collar. The dog started to calm down.

"I'll take him home right away," I said.

"No, you won't," Jenks replied. His smile had vanished. "I have to take him for a rabies test."

"Wowser doesn't have rabies!" I cried.

"We have to make sure," the principal replied. "Leave him with me, Artie. I'll see that he gets home—after the test."

I didn't want to leave Wowser with Mr. Jenks. But I didn't have a choice.

I handed the dog over to him and walked into the school.

I had a heavy feeling in the pit of my stomach. I kept picturing Jenks' bloody hand.

That didn't happen in my dream.

It was worse. Biting his hand was much more serious than ripping his pocket.

Was my *real* first day going to be even more horrible than my dream?

5

I gazed down the long, crowded front hall. Ardmore Middle School was ten times bigger than my old school. The hall stretched for miles with rows of lockers and classrooms down each side.

How would I ever find the gym? Or the lunchroom? Or the boys' room?

The first day in a new school was way tough. And even tougher when you were haunted by a nightmare that kept coming true.

I decided I wouldn't let the rest of that dream ruin my day. No more. No more of it would come true.

Kids pushed and elbowed their way to the wall where the class assignments were posted on computer printouts. I stepped into the crowd and tried to read the long sheets.

"Yo, Brick! Brick!" A tall, skinny boy with spiky blond hair yelled in my ear.

Brick?

The same name as in the dream?

I suddenly felt cold all over.

"Yo, Brick! Whose class are you in?"

"I got Freeley!" The kid named Brick swung around. He looked just like the Brick I had dreamed up. Big and solid and square-shaped. Like a brick in a football jersey. Only good-looking. The jersey had the number "1" on the front and back.

"Hey, I got Freeley, too," the spiky-haired guy said. He and Brick touched knuckles.

Other kids reached their fists out to slap knuckles with Brick. He seemed to be very popular.

Someone pushed me from behind. I stumbled forward—and landed hard on Brick's foot.

"Hey!—" He let out a startled shout. Then he groaned. "Owww. Dude, you're heavier than a feather, you know?" He took a few limping steps.

"S-sorry," I stammered.

The spiky-haired kid stared down at my jeans. "Do you have to use the bathroom or something?"

Kids burst out laughing all around me. I felt my face turning hot.

Brick and his friend started down the hall toward their classrooms. Brick was still limping a little.

"You'd better go apologize to Brick," a voice beside me said.

I turned to see a girl in a bright yellow top and short brown skirt. Shelly. I remembered her from my dream. Yes, of course, I remembered her huge gray-green eyes and straight black hair down to her shoulders.

"You'd better tell Brick you're sorry," she said. "He rules this school."

"I know," I said. *Why did I say that?*

"He's an all-state middle school quarterback," Shelly said. "And he's a brain. And he's a totally good guy. Everyone likes him."

"I like him, too," I said. "I mean, I don't *know* him. But I already like him."

I was trying to be funny. But she squinted at me without laughing.

I guess it wasn't too funny.

"You hurt his foot," Shelly said. "You don't want to get everyone mad at you."

I opened my mouth to answer. But I didn't have a chance.

I heard kids shout a warning—and that baseball came flying in through the front door.

Oh no, I thought. *No way.*

This time, I'm not going to throw the baseball and bean Brick and knock him out.

That is NOT going to come true.

I dodged to the wall—and let Shelly catch the ball. It made a loud *smack* as she trapped it in her hands.

Kids cheered and shouted.

I cheered, too. I was excited. I was finally going to break free of that nightmare.

I heard a shout. "Throw it here! Shelly—toss it!" It was the tall, spiky-haired kid. He stood halfway down the hall next to Brick.

He raised his hands. "Shelly—throw it here!"

Shelly pulled back her arm, preparing to toss the ball.

I waved my hand. "Go! Throw it!" Shouting a little encouragement to her.

Shelly heaved the ball.

It bounced off my hand—changed angles—and sailed down the hall.

It made a very loud *thwoccck* as it hit Brick in the back of the head.

"Ohhhh." A weird moan escaped his throat.

His arms shot straight up. He did a crazy tap dance. Then his knees folded. And he sank to the floor, unconscious.

"Why did you *do* that?" Shelly shrieked at me. "You made it hit Brick! You made it hit him!"

Shuddering in horror, I looked out at a crowd of angry stares.

6

Some kids screamed. Shelly ran down the hall, shouting Brick's name. A big crowd of kids huddled around him on the floor.

He sat up quickly, rubbing the back of his head. His eyes rolled around crazily, then settled down. He blinked several times, then looked in my direction.

"Who threw that ball?" he asked. He sounded groggy. He rubbed his head.

I hadn't moved. I stood frozen in disbelief.

"I threw the ball," Shelly said. "But that new kid hit it. He made it change directions."

Brick squinted at me. "Aren't you the kid who stomped on my foot?"

"Accident," I choked out. "It was all an accident."

Two guys helped Brick to his feet. He seemed dazed but okay.

Mr. Jenks came rushing down the hall. His torn jacket flapped as he ran.

"What's going on?" he demanded. "Why aren't you in class?"

Brick pointed at me. "That new kid hit me with a baseball," he said. "Nearly knocked me out."

Jenks turned to me. Again, his smile had vanished. "You're having a bad morning, Artie," he said. "First your dog might have given me rabies. Then you knock Brick to the floor?"

"Accidents," I said. My voice cracked. My knees suddenly felt shaky. "Accidents. Really."

"Brick, go to the nurse. Let her check you out," Jenks said.

Then he turned back to me and lowered his voice. "Sometimes I take the law into my own hands, Artie," he whispered.

Again, I knew I hadn't heard right. He *couldn't* have said that—could he?

"I'm the law around these parts," Jenks whispered. Again, I smelled peppermint on his hot breath as it brushed my ear. "Don't fight the law. The law always wins."

"Uh . . . okay," I said.

I have to get out of here, I thought. *This is the worst day of my life, and I'm not even in class yet.*

Jenks patted my shoulder. He flashed me a warm smile. "Go get 'em, Otter!" he said.

Huh? Otter?

Then I glimpsed the big glass display case across from us. It was filled with silver sports trophies. A red-and-blue sign above the case read, GO, OTTERS.

Okay. Go, Otters.

Go, Artie, I thought.

I can change this day. I know I can.

I read the class sheet. I was in room 307. Ms. McVie's class.

I remembered the trouble I had in my dream. How I couldn't find the room. How I ended up in the wrong class, sitting in Brick's seat.

Not today, I vowed.

From now on, I change everything.

I saw Shelly across the hall and walked over to her. She studied me with those bright gray-green eyes. I guessed she was trying to decide whether or not to be nice to me.

"What happened to your hair?" she asked.

"Syrup accident," I said. I rolled my eyes. "I have a little brother."

"Me, too," she said. She had a nice laugh.

“This is my first day at Aardvark,” I said. “I’m in your class. Can I walk with you?”

“No worries,” she said. She tossed her long hair over her shoulder. “This school is crazy. I’ll show you where the room is.”

Her backpack was on the floor at her feet.

“I’ll get it,” I said.

We both bent over for it at the same time—and cracked heads.

“Owwww.” We both let out yelps of pain.

I grabbed my head. It felt about to split open.

When I could focus my eyes again, Shelly was waving me away. “Why don’t you go on ahead?” she said. “I think it’ll be safer.”

“But—” I started to protest. I really wanted to stay with her. She could easily lead me to the right room.

But I saw a red bump on her forehead. It swelled up fast, like a balloon inflating. I decided I’d better listen to her and scram.

So I started to wander down the long halls. The room numbers were tiny and etched into the wood doors. Very hard to read.

Everyone was already in class. The halls were empty. No one to ask for help.

The room numbers didn’t make any sense at all. I knew Room 307 should be on the third floor. But the 200 rooms were all mixed together with 300 rooms.

My footsteps echoed on the tile walls. I thought I heard a kid crying. I stopped to listen. Yes. I heard soft sobs.

And then there were more sobs and cries. It sounded like a whole classroom of kids, all wailing and sobbing.

My breath caught in my throat. I stopped outside a door to listen. Why were they all crying so hard? I'd never heard so many people crying at the same time.

It sounded a little like a baby nursery. Only the voices were older—not babies.

I froze and listened through the closed wooden door. I knew something *horrible* must have happened.

Finally, I couldn't hold myself back. The sobs were just too frightening and sad.

I grabbed the brass doorknob with a trembling hand. I pushed open the door.

I peered into the room—and gasped in shock.

7

The room was empty. No one in there.

Silence now. No sobs. Only the shallow sounds of my own rapid breaths.

My whole body shuddered. I gazed wide-eyed at the empty classroom.

The bright ceiling lights were on. I took a shaky step into the room. I stared at the rows of desks. Something glowed on the desktops under the lights.

I reached out and touched the nearest desk. Wet.

The desktop was wet. From tears?

The next desk was also wet. The water was warm. I rubbed my finger through the puddle. Were there teardrops on all the desks?

"This is *too freaky*," I said out loud. My voice came out soft and muffled.

Wiping my wet finger on my jeans, I backed out of the silent, empty room.

Something was wrong here. Something was very wrong in this school.

I backed into the empty hall. My heart was drumming in my chest.

I took a deep breath and started my search for Room 307 again. As I followed the twisting halls, I kept thinking about my dream.

Why did I remember last night's dream so clearly? Why did I remember every single thing that happened?

I was still thinking about it when I spotted a classroom with "307" etched on the door. I studied it carefully. I didn't want to make the same mistake as before.

The bell rang as I stepped into the classroom. It was filled with laughing, talking kids. "Is this sixth grade?" I asked a boy whose dark hair fell over his forehead. He concentrated on sending a text message on his phone.

He nodded without looking up.

I glanced around the room, searching for Ms. McVie. No sign of her. I figured the kids wouldn't be laughing and talking and texting if she were here.

My eyes scanned the desks. They were all taken. Except for one in the back row near the door.

Did that desk belong to Brick?

It couldn't. Not if I was in the right room. And I had checked and double-checked the room number: 307. I knew I was okay this time.

I dropped down behind the empty desk. I lowered my backpack to the floor in front of me. I unzipped it and started to pull out a writing pad.

But I stopped when a shadow fell over me.

I knew it was Brick. I knew this scene was happening again.

I looked up at him. He didn't look happy to see me. Big surprise, right?

He stood over me, his big chest heaving up and down beneath his football jersey.

"Dude, are you *following* me?" he demanded.

"Uh . . . no," I said.

"Then why are you in my seat?" he boomed. "Get up, dude. I don't know what you're trying to prove this morning. But, I'm warning you—get out of my face."

"Okay, okay," I muttered. "Sorry."

I grabbed the strap of my backpack and started to hoist it from the floor. But my hand slipped—and it shot up, right into Brick's face.

“My eye!” he shrieked. He staggered back against the wall. He covered his eye with one hand. “You put out my eye! I can’t see! I can’t *see*!”

That’s when the teacher walked in, followed by Mr. Jenks.

8

"What's going on here?" Mr. Jenks demanded. His cheeks grew pink, and his tiny eyes beamed in on me.

"This kid punched me in the eye," Brick said.

He pulled his hand away from the eye. The eye didn't look too bad. A little red, maybe.

"I asked him to get out of my seat, and he punched me in the eye," Brick said.

Mr. Jenks came striding toward us. "Is this true, Artie?" he asked.

The teacher stayed in the doorway. She was an older woman with short gray hair, pale gray eyes, and gray cheeks. She was dressed in a gray sweater and gray slacks.

It was like she was in one of those old black-and-white movies. Her mouth was frozen in a little *O.* She just stood there, not moving.

"My hand slipped, Mr. Jenks," I said. "It was an accident. Totally."

"Like the accident with the baseball?" Jenks asked, eyeing me suspiciously. His cheeks went from pink to red.

"Yes," I said.

"Like the accident with my suit jacket?"

"Yes," I said.

Mr. Jenks put a hand on Brick's shoulder and turned to me. "We need this guy, Artie," he said. "We need Brick to be healthy. We don't want this guy hurt."

He pushed his nose right up to mine and stared into my eyes. "Get me?"

"Uh . . . yes." I tried to pull my face away, but I was trapped there in the seat.

"Can I have my desk?" Brick asked Jenks.

The principal motioned for me to get up. I grabbed my backpack and climbed out of the desk.

I turned to Brick. I didn't want him to hate me. I didn't want to make an enemy on my first day of school. Especially the most popular guy in the school.

"Brick, I'm totally sorry," I said. "I promise it won't happen again."

I stuck my hand out to shake hands with him. I

swung too fast—and my hand jabbed him hard in the stomach.

Brick grabbed his belly and doubled over.

"Oops. Sorry," I said. "That was an accident. Really."

Holding his stomach, he made an awful groan. Then he started puking his guts out on the desk.

I raised my eyes to Mr. Jenks. "Accident," I said.

Jenks spun away from me. "Will someone go get the janitor?" he cried.

Two girls jumped up and ran out of the room. The teacher still hadn't moved from her spot near the doorway.

Brick must eat a very big breakfast. He had a lot to puke up. He made horrible groans as he did it.

Jenks frowned at me. "I'm watching you, Artie," he said through clenched teeth. "My patience is great. But my wrath is greater. Know what I mean?"

"Not really," I said.

But he didn't hear me. He was already storming to the classroom door. The teacher stepped out of his way as he strode into the hall. Then she started to her desk.

A man in a dark blue work uniform walked in carrying a mop and a pail. "Someone have first-day jitters?" he asked the teacher.

She shrugged. “Not really.”

“Ms. McVie,” I called. “There aren’t enough seats.”

“I’m not Ms. McVie,” she said. “I’m Mrs. Freeley.”

Of course. And I’m in the wrong room. Again.

She picked up her list. “What’s your name?”

“Mud,” I said.

She scanned the page. “You’re not in my class, Mr. Mud.”

“I guess this isn’t Room 307,” I said.

She shook her head. “It’s 307-A. Right across the hall.”

“Sorry,” I said. I grabbed my backpack and started to leave.

But Brick, still wiping his mouth with the back of his hand, grabbed my arm. “Yo, you’re taking my backpack.”

I glanced down. We had the same blue-and-black backpack. “Sorry.” I dropped his and picked up my own.

I could feel his angry eyes on me as I trudged to the door.

You probably think my first day at Aardvark Middle School wasn’t going too well. Yes, you’re totally right.

But I made a promise to myself as I opened the

door to Room 307. I promised myself I was going to change everything.

From now on, I would refuse to make the mistakes I made during my *first* first day.

I took a deep breath and walked up to Ms. McVie. *From now on everything will be different.*

9

Ms. McVie looked exactly as she had the first time. Young and tall with brown hair tied behind her head in a ponytail.

She wore the same big red-plastic eyeglasses. She was even wearing the same brown vest over a white sweater and faded jeans as in my dream the night before.

Weird.

Totally weird.

"Artie, why don't you take that seat by the window," she said. She pointed.

"I really don't want to sit there," I said.

Because I want things to be different this time. Get it?

"Sorry. It's the only open seat," she said. "Does anyone want to trade seats with Artie?"

I gazed around the room. I saw Shelly in the front row. She had a red lump on her forehead.

No hands went up.

"Okay, okay," I muttered. "No worries. Really." I slumped to the desk by the open window.

A sweet-smelling breeze floated into the room. But it didn't make me happy. I had to concentrate hard. Stay alert.

I had to make sure history didn't repeat itself.

Ms. McVie sat on the edge of her desk. She crossed her long legs. "I'm going to tell you about all the things we're going to study this year," she said.

I raised my hand. She squinted at me. "Yes. What is it, Artie?"

"Please don't sit on the desk," I said.

Her mouth dropped open. Several kids laughed.

I felt my face growing hot. I knew I was blushing.

"Artie, are you feeling okay?" Ms. McVie asked.

I nodded. "Yes. But—"

"Well, why don't you want me to sit on the desk? Are you worried about the furniture in this room?"

That made a lot of kids laugh. I saw Shelly laugh, too.

"I just—well . . ."

How could I explain it?

"Artie, I hope you're not going to be trouble," she said. She shifted her legs. "Are you?"

"No," I said.

Then I glimpsed the scorpion in its glass case on the window ledge right beside me. The rare and valuable scorpion. And I remembered so clearly how that bee flew down the back of my shirt. How it made me go crazy. And how I slapped the scorpion out the window, never to be seen again.

"I suppose you're all wondering about that creature in the glass case," Ms. McVie said, pointing in my direction. "It's our class scorpion."

Not for long—unless I do something to change history.

I raised my hand.

Ms. McVie groaned. "*Now* what, Artie?"

"Is it okay if I close the window?" I said. "It's kind of . . . windy here."

"Okay. Go ahead," she said. She turned back to the class. "The scorpion comes all the way from the African desert. It's very rare and worth a lot of money."

And now I'm going to save its life by closing the window.

I stood up, turned, and leaned over the scorpion

cage. I reached up and grabbed the bottom of the window.

Then I tightened my arm muscles and tugged down hard.

The window was tight. It refused to slide.

I gripped the bottom tighter—and pushed down with all my strength.

"Oh!—" I uttered a sharp cry as my hands slipped off the window. I banged the glass top of the scorpion cage. The top flew off.

I heard Ms. McVie scream as she fell off her desk.

The cage toppled over. And the scorpion fell out the window.

"Noooooo!"

A horrified scream escaped my throat.

I couldn't let it fall. I dove for it.

And sailed out the window after it.

10

I dove straight down. Fell two stories, screaming all the way.

Down . . . down . . .

My hands grabbed air. My feet sailed up above me.

Down . . .

I landed on my stomach. My body jerked hard. Bounced once or twice.

My breath shot out of me. I began to choke.

It took a few seconds to realize I'd landed on top of a hedge. A thick evergreen hedge. It felt like a springy mattress. It saved my life.

Slowly, I began to breathe again. The evergreen leaves prickled my face. I lifted my head.

I heard screams from the window high above me. Faces poked out, gazing down at me in horror.

I waved up at them. “Perfect landing!” I shouted. “I’m okay.”

Ms. McVie stuck her head out the window. “Artie?—” She was pale with fright.

“When do I get my pilot’s license?” I cried.

It was easy to joke. I was so happy to be alive and in one piece.

“Artie? Don’t move. I’ll get the nurse,” Ms. McVie called.

I sat up on the top of the hedge. “No, I’m fine. It was a very good flight.”

“Get back up here and let’s take a look at you,” she shouted.

I pressed both hands against the hedge top, pushed myself off, and leaped to the ground.

I landed hard—and heard a sick *squissssh* under my shoes.

Uh-oh.

I had a very bad feeling. I lifted my shoe. My bad feeling was right.

I had crushed the scorpion flat under my shoe.

With a sigh, I picked it up and examined it. Definitely dead. I had crushed the shell under my heel.

“Well, *that* went well,” I said to myself. I tossed the dead scorpion into the hedge.

I tested my legs. I stretched my arms over my head. I felt fine. No pain. No problems.

I started to jog along the hedge to the front of the school building. Birds twittered in the trees. A big yellow hound dog lay on its back on a patch of sunlight. Everything shimmered under the autumn sun.

I turned the corner—and stopped with a gasp. A stream of cold water rushed at me.

I didn't have a chance to dodge away from it. A blue-uniformed gardener looked up in shock as I cried out. He was watering the hedge with a long, green hose. He didn't see me come trotting around the corner.

The hose sent a spray of icy water onto the front of my jeans.

"Oh, noooo!" I wailed. I jumped to the side. Too late.

The front of my jeans was soaked.

"Sorry," the gardener said. "Aren't you supposed to be in school?"

"I just flew in," I said.

I tried to cover the wet spot with my T-shirt. But the shirt wasn't long enough.

A short while later, I stepped back into Ms. McVie's

classroom. Everyone cheered and clapped. It was like I was a hero.

Ms. McVie came limping over to me, a pained smile on her face.

"Why are you limping like that?" I asked.

"I fell off my desk," she said. "I think I hurt my back."

Then she lowered her eyes to the wet stain on the front of my jeans. "Poor Artie," she said. "You really *were* scared, weren't you!"

I started to tell her about the gardener. But I felt a sharp prickle in the middle of my back. Something furry brushed my skin.

Of course, I knew what it was. A bumblebee. It must have flown up my T-shirt while I was sprawled on the hedge.

"Oh, no," I muttered. "Not again."

I was standing in front of the whole class. I saw Shelly staring up at me from her front-row seat.

I twisted my body. Tried to squirm so the bee would fly out the bottom of the shirt.

It buzzed loudly and bumped the back of my shoulder blades. Chills rolled up and down my back.

I thrashed and squirmed. The bee prickled my back again.

I frantically twisted and squirmed. My right hand shot out—and clipped Shelly in the chin.

She groaned. Her gray-green eyes rolled up in her head. She fell off her chair and crumpled to the floor.

"Accident! Accident!" I cried.

When the bee finally stung me, I was too upset to care.

11

Two kids volunteered to help Shelly to the nurse's office. She squinted at me as she left the room. She had a big red bruise on her chin to match the one on her forehead.

Of course, I still had a slight crush on Shelly. But I don't think I was one of her favorite guys.

A short while later, Ms. McVie sent me to the nurse's office to have the bee stinger pulled from my back. The sting made a large bump swell up. The nurse rubbed a lotion on it that made it really burn like crazy.

When I returned to the classroom, Ms. McVie had a pillow on her desk chair. She called me over.

"I don't have enough science textbooks," she said. "I need you to go down to the book room and bring up three or four."

I remembered the book room from my dream. And the creepy fat man who worked down there. I really didn't want to go back there.

"Can't anyone else go?" I asked. "My back kind of hurts. From the bee sting."

"Walk it off," Ms. McVie said. "It just needs exercise."

"No. Really," I said. "Maybe someone else?—"

"I'd like *you* to go," she insisted. "To be perfectly honest, I need the peace and quiet."

She waved me to the door with both hands. "It's in Level Two, in the basement. Mr. Blister will know what books you need. Don't hurry."

I stared at her. "Mr. Blister?"

She nodded. "Get going."

I remembered how scary that book room was. I remembered hiding in the back room after school. And seeing those strange figures all wrapped in gauze.

I didn't want to go down there. But what choice did I have?

I followed the stairs down to the basement. The lights were dim down here. The tile walls were faded and dirt-smeared.

Water pipes ran along the ceiling. Some of them were draped with cobwebs.

I knew where I was headed. I passed the furnace room. Empty and silent. Hot air pipes twisted in all directions.

I walked past several closed doors. My sneakers were covered with dust. I ducked under a thick blanket of cobwebs.

And stopped in front of a half-open door. I heard a groan from inside. It sounded like a man in pain.

A low moan followed. A woman moaning and sighing.

Was someone in there? Someone in trouble?

I took a deep breath. Grabbed the doorknob. Pushed the door all the way open.

And peered into the room. Peered at the rows of crooked tombstones.

A graveyard. Old-looking gravestones, cracked and tilted. They poked up from a thick layer of dirt.

I counted six rows of gravestones. Maybe ten graves in a row.

The lights were dim. The air was cold and smelled sour like dirt and decay. Like a graveyard.

A graveyard in the basement of a middle school?

I heard another groan. A man's low murmur.

The sound sent a chill to the back of my neck.

I took a step into the room. I was stepping on dirt.

I gazed up. The ceiling was high above. A soft wind blew against my face.

From where?

I wasn't outside. I was in the basement. Indoors. Staring at the rows of tombstones. Chipped and broken, their etched words rubbed smooth.

Old graves.

I stood there, gazing without blinking. Trying to make sense of it.

And then . . . something moved.

In the corner of my eye, I caught something moving behind a wide stone at the end of the first row.

"Ohhhhh." A frightened moan escaped my throat. I raised my hands to my mouth.

And gaped in horror as a pale hand reached up. Yes—slowly . . . slowly . . . a pale hand raised itself from the grave.

12

I fell back against the wall. My breath came out in shuddering gasps.

I watched the hand reach up and grab the top of the gravestone. Then I heard another groan.

I saw a man's head raise up. The head was bald and had pointed ears like a *Star Trek* character. The face was pink and round with several flabby chins.

The man's other hand gripped the tombstone. And with another groan, he pulled himself to his feet.

An enormous fat man appeared, wearing a huge, maroon sweatshirt and gray sweatpants. He took a second to catch his breath. Then he saw me.

He blinked, startled. He had one blue eye and one brown eye.

I was still pressed against the wall. I didn't know if I could speak or not. My throat felt tight and dry.

“Sorry if I startled you,” the man said. His voice was soft and distant, as if it was coming from deep inside his huge belly.

He wiped his hands on his sweatshirt. “I try to keep these stones looking nice,” he said. “They’re very old, you know. So it’s a lot of work. I have to get down on my hands and knees.”

I started to recover. At least, my legs stopped shaking. “Are you—” I started.

“Were you looking for me in the book room?” he asked. “I’m Mr. Blister.”

“Y-yes,” I stammered. “Ms. McVie sent me. But—” I gazed at the rows of tombstones. “What are they doing down here? Why are they here? Are there really people buried under those stones?”

He picked up a shovel lying flat on the dirt. He shoved the blade into the dirt. “You’re new, huh?” he said.

I nodded. “Yeah. My name is Artie.”

He studied me. “Well, Artie, didn’t they tell you this school was built on top of a graveyard?”

“N-no,” I stammered.

He nodded. His chins rolled up and down. “Yes, it’s a very old graveyard. Some of the early settlers in this town are buried down here. And they’re not happy about it.”

I swallowed. "What do you mean?"

"Well, it's all a legend," Blister said. "You know. It's a story. You don't have to believe it if you don't want to." He mopped his pink forehead with the sleeve of his sweatshirt.

I waited for him to continue.

"They say the dead people weren't happy about having a school built on top of them," Blister said in his soft voice. "They wanted the cool night air and the song of birds."

He shook his head. "But this was the land granted for a school. It had to be built on this spot. And the graveyard couldn't be moved—by law."

I thought about it. "So how do you know the dead people are so unhappy?" I asked.

"They told me so," Blister replied.

13

"Excuse me?" I swallowed again. Was Blister totally crazy?

"They rise up once a year," he said. "On All Rising Day. They rise up from their graves and go howling through the school. All of them. All rotted and decayed, with their arms and legs falling off, and stinking to high heaven. It's their revenge."

He's a total nut job, I told myself. *I've got to grab those science books and get out of here.*

"When is All Rising Day?" I asked.

He shrugged. "You never know. Could be any day. Could be *today.*"

I stared at him. "You don't know when it happens?"

"No. It's always a surprise. It—" He stopped. He turned to the rows of gravestones, and his eyes bulged in horror. His pink face turned bright red.

"Oh . . . oh . . . oh . . ." he repeated. "Artie, it's *happening*! Look! Here they *come*!"

I gasped. My eyes frantically scanned the graves.

I didn't see them. I didn't see anything moving.

Blister tossed back his head and laughed. A deep, booming laugh that shook his enormous belly.

He laughed till he choked. Then he heaved himself toward the door.

"Guess they're not rising today," he said. He laughed some more.

"You got me," I muttered. "Guess you tell that story to frighten all the new kids."

His smile faded. He narrowed his eyes at me. "Maybe it's a true story," he muttered. "Follow me."

I followed behind him as he lumbered to the book room. His big body bumped the walls as he walked. His stomach bounced up and down like a huge beach ball.

The book room was just as I'd seen it, with bookshelves on all four walls and rows of shelves filling the long room. Blister led me to the wall of TV monitors. I could see a different classroom on each screen.

"What book do you need?" he asked, rubbing his chins.

"Science book for Ms. McVie," I said. "I need three or four of them."

"No problem," he muttered.

He opened the drawer and pulled out a tape measure. He squeezed it in his meaty hand. "Come closer, Artie. You have to be measured for books."

I took a step back. This was too weird.

"I don't want to be measured," I said.

He stared hard at me with his brown eye and blue eye. "School rule," he said. He pulled the tape out a few feet. "Come here, Artie."

Panic tightened every muscle in my body. Why did he want to measure me? I thought about the gauze-wrapped kids in the back room. I remembered the mannequin that said he was Artie.

"No. Really," I said. I stepped back further. "Don't measure me."

"School rule," he insisted. He lurched toward me.

A phone rang on the desk against the wall. Blister turned toward it. He tucked the measuring tape into the pocket of his sweatpants. "Wait there," he said.

He heaved his huge body toward the phone.

I stood frozen. I couldn't decide what to do.

And then all the monitors up and down the wall began to flicker.

I stared in surprise. The classrooms on the screens faded in and out. I heard a low hum. The hum became a strange buzz.

The screens went black. Then white. Then black again.

And then, as I gaped in shock, four words appeared. Four words in dark, blood-red letters flashed onto every monitor screen. . . .

ARTIE, RUN AWAY—NOW.

14

I stared in shock at the frightening red words. Who was sending me a message?

I turned to the desk. Mr. Blister had his back turned. The phone was pressed to his pointy ear.

Should I wait for the science books? Or follow the advice on the screens?

It didn't take me long to decide. I kept my eye on Blister and backed up a few steps. Then I spun around and took off running.

I knew he couldn't catch me. He was too big and slow to run after me.

My shoes kicked up dust as they pounded the concrete floor. I ran down the long low hall. I passed the graveyard with its old crooked stones and kept running.

The big red words on all those monitors stayed in my mind:

ARTIE, RUN AWAY—NOW.

Who could have been warning me? Who knew I was in the book room?

What kind of danger was I in?

My brain was doing flip-flops in my head. I knew I had to think up an excuse for Ms. McVie. I had to think up a good reason for why I didn't get the science books.

I was out of breath by the time I reached the stairs at the end of the hall. My chest was aching.

I stopped to take a breath. And that's when I saw something that changed *everything.*

I raised my hand to wipe sweat off my forehead. And I saw something that made me gasp in shock.

A red burn mark across the palm of my hand.

The burn mark from grabbing the hot steam pipe in the basement hallway.

But I didn't grab the pipe today. I didn't burn myself *today.*

I burned myself *the first time* I came down here—in my dream.

I stood there staring in horror at my hand. What did it mean?

You can't get a burn on your hand from a dream.

The burn was real. I pressed my finger against it, and it hurt.

So what did that mean?

It meant that my first time here *wasn't* a dream. Not a dream. Not a dream. Not a dream.

It really happened.

That first day here at Ardmore Middle School was *real*.

And here I was, back in the first day of school. I was living it for real—a second time. Living the same day all over again.

Only this time, it was much scarier and much more dangerous.

The first day of school had been the worst day of my life. And today, living it for the second time, it was even *scarier*.

Up on the first floor, a long bell rang. The lunch bell. The sound made me jump. I lowered my hand. But I could still see the red burn mark as if it had been branded into my eyes.

I knew if I went up to lunch, I would drop my tray and then bump heads with Shelly. And then I would set things in motion that would make

Brick break his leg. And the whole school would hate me.

I couldn't let that happen again. But as I pulled myself up the stairs, the question kept repeating in my mind:

Is there any way I can stop *it?*

15

"I'll skip lunch," I decided. That would definitely change the day.

I climbed the stairs. Kids jammed the hall. Most of them were heading to the lunchroom.

I hurried to Ms. McVie's room to get my backpack. I peeked into the room first. Luckily, she wasn't in there.

I picked up my backpack and walked toward the lunchroom. I saw Brick and his friend Darnell in the food line.

Outside the entrance, backpacks were tossed in a huge pile. That's what everyone did at lunchtime, I guessed. They just dropped their backpacks outside the lunchroom door.

I tossed mine onto the pile. But I didn't get in line for food. I knew what would happen if I did. Instead, I pushed open a back door and stepped outside.

The sun had disappeared behind high clouds. A cool breeze greeted me as I made my way toward the playground. The air felt nice on my hot cheeks.

My stomach growled.

Sure, I was hungry. But I knew I was doing the right thing. I had to change the afternoon. And lunch was the first thing to be changed.

I walked over the grass and sat down on a swing. I gripped the chains, but I didn't swing myself. The swing was too small. Also, I wanted to think.

It was peaceful out here. I heard a car honk somewhere in the distance. And I heard the soft roar of a lawn mower across the street.

I shut my eyes and tried to think. What exactly was happening to me? And what could I do about it?

I was good at asking the questions. But did I have any answers? No way.

When I opened my eyes, Shelly was sitting in the swing next to mine. She had brushed her hair down to cover the bump on her forehead. But I could still see the red mark on her chin.

"Rough morning?" she said.

I nodded. "Yeah. You could say that."

She opened a brown paper bag and pulled out a sandwich. "Peanut butter without jelly," she said. "Want half?"

I took the half sandwich from her. "Thanks."

"The first day in a new school is always the pits," she said.

"It isn't my first day," I said. My voice trembled. Shelly was the only person in the whole school to be nice to me. I had to tell someone what was happening. I decided to spill everything to her.

"It's my *second* first day," I said. "I already had one first day. I—I don't understand it. But I'm having it all over again."

"Whatever," she said.

"No. I'm serious," I replied. "It's not a joke. I can't figure it out. I mean, it's scary. This day happened already, and—"

"Artie, you're funny," she said.

A gust of wind blew the sandwich bag from her lap. We both bent down to pick it up—and we cracked heads.

"Oww!" she cried out and danced away from the swing. "You're dangerous!" she said, rubbing her head.

"Sorry," I murmured. And then I blurted out, "You hate me—right?"

She stared at me. She didn't answer. "The bell's going to ring. See you later. Stay at least three feet away—okay?"

Before I could reply, she spun away and started to run across the grass toward the school. Her black hair flew behind her head as she ran.

"That went well," I said to myself. I sat there for a while longer. I didn't think of anything useful. Mostly, I thought about Shelly. I guess I already had a major crush on her.

Finally, I walked back into the school building. I felt totally tense. I knew I had to be careful. Careful of everything I did.

I hoisted my backpack from the pile and swung it onto my shoulders. I saw the boys' room across the hall. I pulled open the door and stepped inside.

The lights were so bright, it took a few seconds for my eyes to adjust.

And then the screams began.

And a girl popped her head out from a stall. "You creep!" she cried. "You *creep*! What are you doing in the girls' room?"

I'd totally forgotten. I was thinking so hard about Shelly and Brick, I'd forgotten about walking into the girls' bathroom.

How could I make such a dumb move?

"Sorry," I muttered.

A girl heaved a roll of toilet paper. *Boinnnnng.* It bounced off my forehead.

"Sorry," I repeated.

I backed out of the door—right into Mr. Jenks. The principal uttered a cry as my heel stomped down on his foot.

"Sorry. Accident," I said.

He narrowed his tiny eyes at me. "Did I just see you come out of the girls' bathroom?"

"Accident," I said. "Really."

"Careful, Artie. Be very careful," Jenks said. He shot his hand up and trapped a fly that was buzzing overhead. He closed his fist tight on the fly.

Then he opened his hand to show me the crushed fly. "Careful, Artie. Careful," he repeated. He raised the fly inches from my face. "Be very careful." Then he turned and stomped away.

Weird, I thought. *That dude is definitely weird.*

The second bell rang. I was late for class. I ran up to the second floor. I burst into Ms. McVie's class.

She had her back turned. She was scribbling math problems on the whiteboard.

Shelly didn't look up as I sneaked past her to my seat by the window.

I slid behind the desk. I opened my backpack to get my math notebook. I reached inside—and pulled out . . . a jockstrap.

Oh, no. The wrong backpack *again*.

I raised the jockstrap in front of me. But I remembered what I did the first time this happened. The first time, I shouted, "Hey, this isn't mine!" And everyone in the class turned around to look and laugh.

This time, I was smarter. I held back my surprise. I didn't say a word.

But . . . Ms. McVie's voice rang out. "Artie, what is that? A jockstrap?"

"It isn't mine!" I cried.

The whole class burst into wild laughter.

"Why did you bring that thing to class?" Ms. McVie cried.

"It isn't mine!" I repeated.

More wild laughter.

I turned to see Brick. Just like the first time, he stood over me, scowling furiously as I held the jockstrap in the air.

"You're in a world of trouble, dude. Give me that," he said through gritted teeth. "Now!"

I tried to swing it over to him. But I swung it too hard.

And it flew out the open window.

"Oh, noooooo!" I cried.

I don't know what made me do it. I didn't even think about it.

I dove after it. And, screaming my head off, I went sailing headfirst out the open window—*again.*

I fell fast . . . plunged straight down . . . so fast my scream seemed to float above me.

This time I didn't land in the hedge.

DAY ONE

1

I woke up in my own bed.

The alarm went off. The loud buzz startled me, and I fell out of bed. My head hit the floor. The pain made me clamp my eyes shut.

No. Wait, I thought. *Wait.*

I didn't move I just stayed there on my stomach on the floor, eyes shut.

I can't be back home. The school day isn't over.

I didn't finish the afternoon. I didn't break Brick's leg. I didn't get chased into the book room closet by Darnell and the angry football players.

I opened my eyes. Mom walked into the room. "Artie, did you sleep on the floor?"

"No," I groaned. I pulled myself up. "I fell out of bed again."

She squinted at me. "Again? Did you fall out of bed before?"

"Uh . . . yeah," I said. I shifted my pajamas. I scratched my hair. "Mom, can I talk to you? I mean, for serious?"

She glanced at the clock on my bed table. "Well, yes. If it's short. You don't want to be late on your first day of school." She started to pick up dirty clothes from the floor.

"Mom, it isn't the first day of school," I said. I handed her a pair of balled-up jeans I'd tossed under the bed.

She turned to look at me. "Yes, it is. Of course, it's the first day."

I sighed. "Mom, it's the *third* day of school," I said. "I mean, it's the third *first* day."

She put a hand on my forehead. "You feel okay?"

"Mom, please!" I pleaded. "Just listen to me. I'm not sick and I'm not crazy. But something very weird is happening to me."

"You don't have to shout," Mom said. "Artie, you always get so worked up. What is wrong? Go ahead. I'm listening." She shifted the bundle of clothes in her hand.

"I'm trapped in time or something," I said,

speaking each word slowly and clearly. “I keep living the same day—the first day of school—over and over.”

Mom twisted up her face. “I don’t know about that, Artie. If that was true, I think I’d remember it. Don’t you?”

“Well, no—” I started.

Mom tilted her head. “Living the same day over and over? Didn’t we see that movie together one night?”

I let out a frustrated groan. “Mom, it isn’t a movie. It’s my *life*!”

“Artie, take a deep breath,” she said.

I *hated* it when she said that. And she said it a lot.

“This happens to people all the time,” Mom said. “It’s called déjà vu. You think something happened before, but it didn’t.”

She patted my shoulder. “You know what’s up, Artie. It’s your first day in a new school, and you’re very nervous about it.”

I took a deep breath, just as she instructed. Then I said, “Mom, I’ll prove I was in school already.”

I held up my hand. “See this burn mark? I burned my hand on a steam pipe in the basement at school. I did it on the first first day.”

Mom tucked the bundle of clothes under one arm. She took my hand and examined it. “What burn mark?” she said.

I pulled my hand away and studied it. The burn mark was *gone*. The skin was perfectly smooth.

"You're nervous about your new school," Mom said. "And you're nervous about your dentist appointment after school."

She turned and started toward the hall. "Hurry. Get downstairs for breakfast. Eddy is already there."

"Mom, wait—" I chased after her. "Give me a chance to prove it. I'll tell you everything that's going to happen, okay? If I predict everything, will you believe me that I've lived this day already?"

"If you predict everything?" Mom said. "Sure. Go ahead. Then I'll believe you." She turned around in the doorway. "But let me ask you one question. Were you watching the Syfy channel before you went to sleep last night?"

I groaned again. "Mom, this has nothing to do with the Syfy channel. It's really happening to me. You'll see."

She headed downstairs with the dirty clothes. I already knew what I'd wear to school. I'd worn it two times.

I glanced at my phone on my desk. I knew if I plugged it into the charger, I'd get a major shock. So I ignored it this morning.

I pulled on my T-shirt and jeans and raced

downstairs. My heart was pounding. I felt kind of breathless.

I was really eager to prove to Mom what was happening. I just had the feeling that if she believed me, she could stop it somehow.

Sure enough, Dad had already left for work. Wowser was in his usual place under the table. And Eddy was already sitting there, gobbling down a stack of toaster waffles.

"Good morning, Piggy," I said to him.

He burped in reply. I knew he would.

Mom was at the coffeemaker, pouring herself a mug of coffee.

"Mom, here's what's going to happen," I said. "I'm going to sit down across from Eddy. He's going to spill his orange-juice glass. Then, we're both going to reach for the waffle syrup at the same time. And he's going to squirt syrup on my hair and my T-shirt."

Mom frowned at me.

"Just watch," I said. "Trust me."

I stepped over to the table and started to slide in across from Eddy. But I stopped halfway into my seat. I stared at Eddy's plate. He wasn't eating waffles.

"Mom?" I called. "Where are the waffles?"

"We're not having waffles," Mom said. "I made scrambled eggs."

Huh?

My breath caught in my throat. My mind spun. "Mom? Did we have waffles *yesterday*?" I asked.

She shook her head. "We had cereal yesterday."

I slid into my seat. Mom scooped eggs onto my plate. I gazed at Eddy. Time for him to spill his orange juice. But, whoa—

Eddy was drinking milk. He picked up the glass and gulped it all down. Then he stuck out his white tongue at me.

"Can I have ketchup on my eggs?" Eddy demanded.

Mom brought a ketchup bottle to the table. She started to pour some onto Eddy's eggs. But he grabbed the bottle. "No! I want to do it!"

"Fine," Mom said. She turned and walked out of the kitchen.

Eddy picked up the plastic ketchup bottle. I saw the evil grin on his face. But I didn't have time to move. He squeezed it hard and sprayed a huge blob of ketchup on my face.

The ketchup ran down my forehead, down my cheeks, and dripped onto my T-shirt. "Aaaaiiii!" I let out an angry scream.

Mom came running back into the room. "What's the problem?"

Her eyes bulged when she saw me. "Artie—you're bleeding! You're bleeding!"

Eddy tossed back his head and giggled like an idiot.

"It's ketchup, Mom," I groaned. "He squirted me."

Mom glanced up at the clock. "Go change your shirt. You have to walk Eddy to his school. I'll tie Wowser up in the backyard."

"Tie him up good," I told her. "So he doesn't rip Mr. Jenks' pocket off."

She squinted at me. "What are you *talking* about? You don't make any sense. Are you sure you feel okay?"

"I'm okay," I said. "But are you sure this is the first day of school?"

She rolled her eyes. "Yes, I'm sure, Artie," she said. "Please don't ask me again. Go ahead. Hurry. Get changed."

I ran upstairs and washed the ketchup off my face. Then I changed my T-shirt. This was all very disturbing. It was the first day of school—but things were different.

I was still trapped on the same day. But I couldn't prove it to Mom.

Did this mean the whole day would be different? Did it mean my first day at Aardvark Middle School would be *better*?

Eddy and I stepped out of the house. It had rained the night before. Just like the first times, Eddy jumped through the puddles like a chimpanzee, splashing up waves of cold water.

When we reached the corner across from his school, I suddenly had a heavy feeling in the pit of my stomach. I knew what was coming. The long, silver gasoline truck, roaring toward us to splash my jeans.

I gazed down the street. I saw the big truck turn the corner a few blocks away.

I grabbed Eddy by the shoulders. "Move!" I shouted. "Back up!"

"No!" Eddy cried. He twisted out of my grasp. He danced away from me.

The truck honked its horn—a long blast—as it approached.

It rumbled closer. I could read the letters on the side of the big tank.

Wait! It didn't say GASOLINE.

In big, black letters along the side of the silver tank, it said, SKUNK OIL.

"Eddy—BACK UP!" I screamed.

Too late. The big truck hit a hard bump. I saw a metal cap fly off the top of the tank.

A tall wave of dark yellow liquid spouted high into the air.

And splashed down over me. Drenching me.

The truck roared past. My whole body shuddered. I shook liquid off me. It poured down my hair . . . my face . . .

It took a few seconds for the smell to reach my nose. When I finally smelled myself, I gasped—and started to retch.

"Ohh, you stink!" Eddy cried, holding his nose and dancing away. "You *stink*!"

It was the sourest, sickest, most gut-wrenching, stomach-churning smell I had ever smelled.

I dropped to my knees in the wet grass. I tried to hold my breath, but it didn't help.

The smell was *inside* me!

"Artie, are you okay? Are you okay?" Eddy's voice sounded far away.

"No," I choked out.

Then everything went black.

DAY ONE

1

I opened my eyes. I blinked a few times. I studied the ceiling, the green-and-white wallpaper.

I was back in bed. Back in my room.

I sniffed hard. I smelled okay. I didn't reek of skunk oil.

The alarm went off. It startled me, and I fell out of bed.

Not again!

"What's going on?" I muttered to myself. "That last time, I didn't even make it all the way to school."

Before I could climb to my feet, Mom came into the room. "Artie, are you talking to yourself?" she asked.

"Yes," I said.

"Why?" she demanded.

"No one else here," I said. I climbed to my feet. "Mom, what day is it? Please tell me it isn't Monday."

She squinted at me. "You know what day it is. It's the first day of school."

I groaned.

She started to gather up dirty clothes from the floor. "Get dressed, Artie. I think you're going to like your new school."

"I don't think so," I murmured. "Really—"

I couldn't finish my sentence. Something strange happened.

The room kind of flickered and flashed. Then all the colors started to spin around me—so fast I couldn't see anything at all. Like I was standing in the middle of a whirling cyclone.

When the colors stopped spinning, I gasped and gazed around. I wasn't in my room any longer. I was outside. I saw kids hurrying up a steep flight of stone steps.

School. I was standing in front of Ardmore Middle School. Gazing up the steps at the man in the brown suit greeting everyone at the front door. Mr. Jenks.

I skipped breakfast. I skipped walking Eddy to his school. I skipped the silver-tank truck.

How could this happen?

It was still the first day of school. But I had skipped about an hour of my life.

I shook my head, trying to clear it. I saw two kids tossing a baseball back and forth at the bottom of the steps.

I adjusted the baseball cap over my hair. Then I climbed the stairs to the school entrance.

"Welcome to Ardmore," Mr. Jenks said. He flashed me a warm smile and shook my hand. I noticed he had a little flag pin on the lapel of his brown suit.

"You need to find whose class you are in," he said. "The class lists are posted on the wall in front of my office."

I know. I know.

The baseball got away from one of the kids. It bounced halfway up the stairs. A girl picked it up and tossed it back to them.

"Careful down there," Mr. Jenks called. "You don't want to hit anyone."

I started to step past Mr. Jenks into the school. But he put a hand on my shoulder to stop me.

"Artie, I'm sorry," he said. "We don't wear baseball caps in this school. Could you please remove yours and hand it to me?"

"Uh . . . sure," I said. I tugged off the cap. Was my

hair sticky with syrup? No. I handed the cap to Mr. Jenks.

To my surprise, he turned it upside down and spit into it. Then he grabbed it in both hands—and ripped the cap in two.

He handed the two pieces back to me with that same smile on his face. "Who is the law, Artie? Who is the law? I am the law!" He pumped a fist in the air.

"Okay. Whatever," I said under my breath.

Holding the two halves of my cap in front of me, I stepped into the school. I saw the crowd of kids bunched in the hall, eager to read the class assignments.

But before I could take a step toward them, I heard shouts behind me on the front steps. I heard a dog bark.

Of course, I knew what was happening. Wowser returns!

I turned back to the school entrance just as the scream began. The most horrifying, painful scream I've ever heard.

I wanted to cover my ears. It took me a while to realize it was Mr. Jenks uttering that horrible animal wail.

Then I saw Wowser. And I saw the hand dangling limply between Wowser's teeth.

Just a hand.

I raised my eyes and saw Mr. Jenks screaming and twisting. He had his arm raised in front of him. I saw the stump on the end of it.

He was swinging the stump wildly. And shrieking: “MY HAND! THE DOG BIT OFF MY HAND!”

2

I dove out the door. I tried to grab Wowser. But the big dog dodged away from me. I dropped to my knees to keep from falling down the stairs.

Wowser raced down the stairs, past screaming kids. And disappeared down the steet, running hard. I could see Mr. Jenks' hand dangling from the dog's jaws.

Mr. Jenks took off after the dog. He ran screaming after Wowser. "Give me my hand! Give it! Give it back!"

Not a great way to start your first day in a new school.

I clamped my eyes shut tight. Could I wake up in my own bed again? Could I have a do-over?

Slowly, I opened them. No. I was still here at the school entrance.

I knew I was in major trouble. I knew I'd be called into the office soon.

But I decided to go on with the day. I had to get all the way through the first day of school. It was the only way that maybe . . . maybe . . . I could go on to the *second* day of school.

So I walked up to the crowd of kids who were studying the lists posted on the wall. I saw Brick and Darnell and Brick's other friend, the kid with the spiky hair. I started to push closer to the class lists—when I heard a shout.

"Look out!"

I turned in time to see the baseball come flying down the hall.

I knew it was going to hit Brick in the back of the head. I tried to stop it. I reached up—grabbed at it. Missed.

The ball rocketed past me—*and shot right through Brick's head!*

The hall filled with gasps and moans and shrieks of horror.

The ball drove right through his skull and out the other side. Brick stood there, frozen stiff, with a hole in his head. A hole the size of a baseball.

I pressed my hands over my ears to keep out the

wails and screams of everyone. I stared at the gaping hole in the back of Brick's skull.

Slowly, he turned around. His eyes were wide with fury. His jaw shook. He raised a hand and touched the hole in his forehead.

He narrowed his eyes at me. "Did you throw that ball?"

"N-no!" I stammered. "I—"

He pointed a finger at me. His eyes rolled crazily in his head. His jaw worked up and down. "Have you seen *Revenge of the Man with the Hole in his Head*?" he demanded.

"Uh . . . no," I choked out.

"That's because you're going to *live* it!" he screamed.

He stared hard at me for a long time. His friends stared at me, too. Then Brick turned and led them away, trudging together down the hall.

I backed against the wall and watched them go. I could see *right through* Brick's head.

What was happening?

Okay, okay. I was living the first day of school all over again.

But why had it suddenly become a *horror show*?

3

I didn't go to the wrong classroom. I went straight to Ms. McVie's room. I stopped outside the door.

"I have to do this differently," I told myself. "I have to take charge."

I stepped into the room. Shelly smiled at me from her seat in the first row. I told Ms. McVie who I was.

"Artie, take that seat by the window," she said, pointing.

I gazed at the open window. I saw the glass case on the window ledge. And I saw the scorpion tapping the glass with one of its claws.

I stepped up to the window, but I didn't take my seat. Instead, I carefully lifted the lid off the glass case and set it down on the ledge.

"Artie, what are you doing?" Ms. McVie called. Everyone stared at me.

"I know you're not going to believe me," I said. "But I've been in this class before. More than once. And I always accidentally knock the scorpion out the window."

The teacher took a few steps toward me. "Please—put that lid back on, Artie. That's a very valuable creature."

"I don't want to have any more accidents with it," I said. I wrapped my hand around its hard body and lifted it from the case.

"Artie! Stop!" Ms. McVie screamed. "What are you going to do?"

"I have to do something different," I said. "Something to change the day."

I raised the scorpion high. Pulled back my arm. And prepared to toss it out the window.

"Noooooo!" Shouts and screams rang out all around me.

They didn't understand. They didn't know how important this was for me.

I swung my arm—and gasped as the scorpion claw closed on my nose.

I tugged. But the scorpion clung to me. The claw tightened on my nose.

"Hey—" I uttered a startled cry.

How did this happen?

The scorpion pinched hard. Pain shot over my face and spread down my whole body. My hand dropped away from the creature. But it clung to my nose, swinging its body from side to side.

And as I cried out in pain, the scorpion began to grow.

I grabbed its body and tried to tug it off. I could feel it start to swell up under my hand. The scorpion quickly inflated like a balloon.

"Help me! Help—somebody!" My cries were muffled by the giant, hard body of the growing creature.

The claws were bigger than my arms! It wouldn't let go of my nose.

I toppled to my back, wriggling in pain. Struggling to push the heavy thing off me.

It weighed a ton. It was bigger than a Great Dane!

"Ohhh . . . Help."

It swiped its enormous claw, ripping off my nose.

I couldn't breathe. The heavy beast was smothering me. Crushing me beneath its massive weight. Crushing me . . .

Crushing me into darkness.

4

When the darkness lifted, I was standing in the hall in front of my locker.

The hall was crowded with kids. Lockers slammed. Everyone laughed and shouted.

Was it lunch break? Or was the school day over? How did I get out here?

I felt my nose. Perfectly okay. But that didn't make any sense.

I didn't have time to think about it. I saw Darnell storming down the hall with a whole posse of angry-looking dudes.

"There he is!" Darnell shouted, pointing at me. "There's the guy who put a hole in Brick's head. Get him!"

Some kids screamed and ducked out of the way as Darnell and his pals came rushing at me.

I froze for a second. I was still thinking about the giant scorpion monster.

Then I finally swung into action. I turned and ran. A group of cheerleader girls blocked the hall. I lowered my head and dove right through them.

"Don't let him get away!" Darnell shouted.

My shoes pounded the hard floor. My heart drummed in my chest as I ran.

I reached the stairs and peered down. I could hear their angry shouts and stampeding feet close behind me.

I grabbed the metal railing and raced down the stairs, taking them two at a time. Could I find a hiding place in the basement? I *had* to.

The light grew dim and the air steamy as I stepped into the basement. The pipes overhead churned. Cobwebs shimmered in the eerie yellow light.

I plunged down the narrow hall. Past the dark, closed doors. My shoes kicked up dust. The dust made me cough and choke. But I kept running.

Into the walled-in graveyard. Yes. I could hide here. My eyes scanned the rows of ancient, cracked, and crumbling gravestones.

Two of them leaned against each other. I dove behind them and hunkered down.

I heard the stampeding football players rumble past. They didn't even slow down.

I grabbed onto the stones with both hands. Waited there, breathing hard. Hunched behind them. I pressed my hot face against the cool stone.

Now what? Where do I run?

I heard a low moan.

Startled, I let go of the gravestone.

Another, longer moan. Then, moans and groans and low cries all around me.

I stood up. I gazed down the row of jagged tombstones.

I saw a hand rise up from behind the stone at the end. It lifted itself slowly, shaking off dirt.

"Mr. Blister?" I called. "Is that you? Are you working here?"

The only reply was a long howl, an animal howl of pain.

And another hand poked up from the dirt right next to me.

I stumbled back. I saw hands rising from the dirt. A dozen hands. No—more. Shaking off dirt. Bare arms poking up.

And then a hideous, rotted face. Mostly just a skull with chunks of meaty flesh clinging to it.

The howls and moans grew louder. I covered my ears and stumbled toward the door.

I gaped in horror as the rotting corpses climbed up from the dirt. They were mostly skeletons with hunks of skin and decaying rags clinging to them.

They shook themselves. An arm fell off one of them and clunked to the dirt. Another corpse held its head in front of it in both hands.

"Noooooo!"

That scream came from my throat as the terrifying bodies began to come at me. They moved slowly, stiffly, groaning and moaning through their toothless mouth holes.

I spun away. I staggered out the door.

Their bones rattled and clicked and snapped as they stumbled after me.

I lowered my head and ran through the dust-choked basement. The hall turned, and I followed it. The howls of the dead people rang in my ears.

All Rising Day.

It is All Rising Day.

I saw the book room at the end of the hall.

Where were the angry football players? Waiting for me in the book room?

I didn't care. I had to get away from the howling, moaning corpses behind me.

I darted into the book room. My eyes gazed around the walls of shelves. “Mr. Blister?” I called breathlessly.

No sign of him.

The wall of monitors was dark.

I knew where I wanted to hide. In the little room behind the back wall. Maybe I'd be safe there. Maybe no one would look for me behind all the high bookshelves.

Gasping for breath, I hurtled through two rows of bookshelves to the back wall. I found the door to the back room and pulled it open.

I plunged inside and closed the door after me. I fumbled on the wall for the light switch and flipped it.

A bright ceiling light flashed on. Still struggling to catch my breath, I spun around. And stared at the figures that filled the tiny room. Figures about my height, all wrapped in gauze.

Were they statues? Mannequins?

I heard moans and howls outside the door. Did the corpses know I was back here?

I froze in panic. If they opened the door, I'd be trapped.

I had to press myself in behind the gauze-covered figures. I could hide in the middle of them.

I raised my hands to push two of them apart. And one of them spoke:

"I'm Artie. I'm Artie."

I jumped back in shock.

The gauze started to move. It slid off the mannequin's head.

"I'm Artie. I'm Artie. Who are you? I'm Artie!"

And as the gauze fell away, I stared at the face in front of me—*my* face!

It had my face. And it had my voice. "Artie. I'm Artie. I'm Artie."

"Noooo!" I couldn't hold back my scream.

And as I screamed, the gauze rolled away on all the other mannequins.

And they *all* looked like me.

I pressed my back against the door and stared in horror at the room full of Arties.

"I'm Artie. Who are you? I'm Artie." They all began to chatter at once.

In my panic, I shoved open the door. I had to get out of there. I had to get away from them.

I stumbled back into the book room.

And saw the decaying, skeletal corpses closing in on me from the aisle between two shelves.

I whirled around. Which way could I run?

The chattering mannequins with my face staggered

behind me. The corpses lurched forward in front of me.

I was trapped between them.

Then I saw Darnell and the football players run into the front of the room. Their eyes searched the aisles, looking for me.

I wanted to cover my head. Shrink down to the floor.

How could I escape? The corpses, the talking mannequins, the angry football players—they all wanted *me*!

My eyes frantically searched around. Was there something I could use as a weapon? Something I could use to fight them off?

No. Just books. Hundreds of books.

Then through the aisle, I saw Mr. Blister lumber into the room. He stood scratching his bald head, watching the strange crowd. Even across the room, I could see the puzzled expression on his face.

"Mr. Blister!" I called. "Can you help me? Mr. Blister?"

"Is that you, Artie?" he shouted.

"I'm Artie!" the mannequins cried. "I'm Artie. I'm Artie!"

I took off, running toward him. I lowered my shoulder and bumped the skeletal corpses out of my way. I ran right through them. Arms dropped off. Heads toppled to the floor.

"Mr. Blister—can you help me?"

I raced up to him, my heart pounding.

He didn't answer. He just stared at me with that puzzled look on his face as I came running up.

The football players surrounded us. The remaining corpses staggered around them. The chattering mannequins joined the crowd.

They formed a tight circle around us. I knew that Mr. Blister was my only chance of surviving.

"Mr. Blister?—Please?" I uttered.

And then something happened to Mr. Blister's huge body.

His belly started to bounce and roll up and down. His shoulders raised and his arms began to curl and uncurl—like snakes.

His bald head rolled back as his stomach shook and quaked under his tight sweatshirt.

"Wh-what's happening?" I stammered.

And then his huge body fell apart. I mean, pieces started to drop off his stomach and sides.

I gaped in shock as big lumps of flesh fell off his stomach.

And then I saw that they weren't lumps. They

were animals. Flesh-colored weasels or some kind of long rat.

The animals slid off Mr. Blister's stomach and plopped to the floor.

"You—you're not human!" I choked out.

His whole body was made of animals! Animals pressed together tightly.

And now the weasel-like creatures were dropping off him, sliding off the big body. They plopped to the floor and scurried away.

I watched in horror as Mr. Blister vanished completely. The last of the pale, furless weasels scrambled across the floor.

Now I was all alone in the center of the corpses and mannequins and angry kids.

They closed in on me silently.

I raised my hands to fight them off.

And then I used my arms to shield myself as they covered me . . . covered me in darkness.

5

When the darkness lifted, I stared into bright light.

I shut my eyes again.

I heard a woman's voice. "I think he's coming out of it."

Then I heard my mother. "Oh, good. Artie? Are you waking up?"

Huh? Waking up?

I opened my eyes again. Used my hand to shield them from the glare.

Was I back in my bed? Was my day starting all over again?

No. I was stretched out in a chair. Leaning back. A long fluorescent light above me. A sink next to the chair.

Dr. Wolfe poked her face over me. My dentist. "He's awake," she said.

My mother's face appeared next to hers. "Artie? You did fine. Your dentist appointment is over."

I blinked. "Dentist appointment?"

Dr. Wolfe smiled down at me. She tugged off her white face mask and brushed back her brown hair. "Sorry, Artie. I didn't think that gas would knock you out for so long. But you should be perfectly fine by dinnertime."

The gas? Yes. It started to come back to me. My dentist appointment. She gave me gas to put me asleep.

"Whoa," I said. I shook my head. I felt dizzy and strange.

Dr. Wolfe laughed. "Artie, did you have weird dreams while you were out?"

I nodded. "Uh . . . yeah. I had a *majorly* weird dream."

The dentist nodded. "Yeah. Patients say they have the most crazy dreams under gas," she said.

"I had a totally crazy dream," I said. I let out a long sigh. "I'm sooo glad it was just a dream."

"Do you remember it?" Dr. Wolfe asked.

"Yes. I kept dreaming the same day over and over," I told her. "And the day got more and more horrifying."

"Interesting," Dr. Wolfe said.

"Let's get you home," Mom said, tugging my arm. "You can tell me your dream in the car."

"I don't think so," I said. "I don't want to talk about it."

I pictured the rotting corpses . . . the flesh-colored animals sliding off Mr. Blister's fat body.

"I just want to forget all about it," I said. "It's over. It's *all* over!"

Wowser was glad to see me when I got home. And I was glad to see him—without a hand dangling from his mouth.

My teeth hurt pretty bad. But Mom made spaghetti for dinner, and I was able to slurp it down easily.

That night, I slept really hard. Sometimes I wake up early in the morning and can't get back to sleep. But I didn't have that problem.

When the alarm went off at seven, the noise startled me. I fell out of bed.

I landed hard on the floor and smacked my head on the edge of the bed.

"Owww."

I was still rubbing my head when Mom walked in. "What are you doing down there?" she asked.

"Doing my morning exercises," I said. "The first

part of my workout is falling. The second part is getting up."

"Very funny," Mom said. She started to collect dirty clothes from my floor. "You don't have time for exercise, Artie. It's the first day of school."

"Huh?" I jumped to my feet. "What did you say?"

"It's the first day of school," she repeated. "I don't have to tell you that. Now, hurry up. Get dressed. You don't want to be late your first day in a new school."

My mouth dropped open. I stared at her. "I don't go on to the *second* day? It . . . it's really starting *again*?"

6

"Chris, is that game player melted to your hand?" Dad said. "You've been playing for hours."

I pressed pause.

"It's an awesome game, Dad," I said. "I almost beat Level One."

He dropped onto the couch next to me, spilling some of his Coke, but he didn't seem to notice. "What kind of a game is it, Chris?" he asked, gazing at the screen. "A war game?"

"No," I said. "It's a different kind of game. It's called First Day of School Forever."

"And what do you have to do?" Dad asked. "How do you play it?" He took the controller from my hand and studied it.

"Well first you pick an avatar," I explained. "I picked this guy Artie."

“That means you control Artie in the game?” Dad asked.

I nodded. “Yeah. I’m Artie. And see, Artie goes to a new school. It’s his first day. And all kinds of weird things happen to him. And I have to get Artie through his first day of school.”

“Sounds easy,” Dad said. He handed back the controller.

“No. Not so easy,” I said. “All kinds of bad things happen to Artie. Sometimes there are monsters and giant scorpions and zombies and things. Sometimes he doesn’t even *survive* the first day, and you have to start the day all over again.”

Dad nodded. “And you almost beat it?”

“Yeah,” I said. “I got him all the way to his dentist appointment after school. But then the first day started all over again. I have to try again. You know. Try something new.”

“Sounds like fun,” Dad said. “Show me.” He took a sip of his drink and stared at the TV screen.

I pressed the play button.

“Okay, watch,” I said. “Watch what happens when Artie’s dog follows him to school. Watch, Dad. This is a riot.”

GOFISH

QUESTIONS FOR THE AUTHOR

R. L. STINE

What did you want to be when you grew up?
I wanted to be a cartoonist and draw comic books. But I quickly discovered I had no drawing talent whatsoever.

Were you a reader or a non-reader growing up?
At first, I read only comic books. Then I discovered sci-fi stories by Ray Bradbury. I started reading all the sci-fi stories I could find.

When did you realize you wanted to be a writer?
When I was nine. I'd stay in my room typing stories and joke magazines. I never wanted to go outside and play. I was a weird kid.

What's your most embarrassing childhood memory?
Throwing up on the school bus. I was in second grade. I heaved right down the aisle. They had to send for a new bus.

What's your favorite childhood memory?
Going fishing with bamboo poles in a river with my dad. He never had much time to spend with us kids. The fishing days were special, even though we never caught anything.

As a young person, who did you look up to most?
The cartoonists who did *MAD* comics and all the EC Horror Comics. I thought they were brilliant and pored over their work like someone viewing masterpieces in a museum.

What was your favorite thing about school?
I wasn't much of a student. I was bored in school. I wanted to be home, writing stories and drawing comics.

What was your least favorite thing about school?
Gym class. I was terrible in all sports. I dreaded gym class every time.

What were your hobbies as a kid? What are your hobbies now?
I don't have time for hobbies. But remember, I live in New York City. The city is a wonderful, exciting show. You only need hobbies if you live somewhere else.

What was your first job, and what was your "worst" job?
My first job when I arrived in NYC was writing for six movie fan magazines. I made up interviews with the stars all day long. I never actually interviewed anyone. I just made it all up. Very creative work.

What book is on your nightstand now?
I'm reading a Robert B. Parker Spenser novel. Also, *Hyperion* by Dan Simmons.

How did you celebrate publishing your first book?
My first book was called *How to Be Funny*. I had a big book signing in the old Doubleday bookstore on Fifth Avenue. And

NO ONE came. No one had ever heard of me. It wasn't much of a celebration.

Where do you write your books?
In my apartment. I have an office I share with a skeleton, several dummies, and my dog.

What sparked your imagination for *It's the First Day of School . . . Forever!*?
I love the idea of someone trapped in a horrifying situation that keeps getting more and more horrifying.

What challenges do you face in the writing process, and how do you overcome them?
My main challenge is how to be scary for kids without being *too* scary. I solve it by using a lot of teasing and humor in the books to lighten things up.

Which of your characters is most like you?
None, I hope.

What makes you laugh out loud?
Laurel & Hardy films. I can watch the same one ten times and still laugh just as hard. I have a very large library of L & H films.

What do you do on a rainy day?
Write, of course.

What's your idea of fun?
I love hanging out with my wife, my son, and his wife. I love going on beach vacations. I love crowded insane places like Disney World and Atlantis in the Bahamas.

What's your favorite song?
"Skylark." It's by Johnny Mercer and Hoagy Carmichael.

Who is your favorite fictional character?
Bertie Wooster and Jeeves in the P.G. Wodehouse novels. I'm a Wodehouse fanatic.

If you could travel in time, where would you go and what would you do?
I would love to go back to NYC in the 1880s. It was portrayed so romantically in Jack Finney's book, *Time and Again*. It was a great, exciting time in the city. For example: There were twice as many theaters in New York in 1880 as there are today.

What's the best advice you have ever received about writing?
Keep it as simple as possible.

Do you ever get writer's block? What do you do to get back on track?
I don't have time for writer's block. Too many books to write! I do a tremendous amount of planning and outlining before I sit down to write. That makes it nearly impossible to have writer's block.

What do you want readers to remember about your books?
I want them to remember that they were overall entertaining and fun, and made reading a fun experience.

What do you consider to be your greatest accomplishment?

Terrifying several generations of kids. Also: encouraging millions of kids to discover the joy of reading.

What would your readers be most surprised to learn about you?

That I love opera and ballet (and country music).

SQUARE FISH